I0817947

ONLY RAGE

(A Sadie Price FBI Suspense Thriller—Book 2)

Rylie Dark

Rylie Dark

Debut author Rylie Dark is author of the SADIE PRICE FBI SUSPENSE THRILLER series, comprising six books (and counting); the MIA NORTH FBI SUSPENSE THRILLER series, comprising three books (and counting); and the CARLY SEE FBI SUSPENSE THRILLER, comprising three books (and counting).

An avid reader and lifelong fan of the mystery and thriller genres, Rylie loves to hear from you, so please feel free to visit www.ryliedark.com to learn more and stay in touch.

ISBN: 978-1-0943-9328-5

BOOKS BY RYLIE DARK

SADIE PRICE FBI SUSPENSE THRILLER

ONLY MURDER (Book #1)
ONLY RAGE (Book #2)
ONLY HIS (Book #3)
ONLY ONCE (Book #4)
ONLY SPITE (Book #5)
ONLY MADNESS (Book #6)

MIA NORTH FBI SUSPENSE THRILLER

NO WAY OUT (Book #1)
NO WAY BACK (Book #2)
NO WAY HOME (Book #3)

CARLY SEE FBI SUSPENSE THRILLER

NO WAY OUT (Book #1)
NO WAY BACK (Book #2)
NO WAY HOME (Book #3)

CHAPTER ONE

"Let's see what we've got here, then," Raul muttered to himself as he approached the hold. He could hear the scuttling and rustling of the crabs underneath. He had seen some beasts out there this season, with legs as long as a child's and pincers that you wouldn't want to mess with. Almost prehistoric looking.

The fisherman opened the hatch that led down into his hold, a half-smile on his face. So far this winter, the catches had been good. Making a living as a crab fisherman wasn't always easy, but something out there had been smiling on Raul recently and the ocean just kept on giving.

It would be a good Christmas. He might even be able to afford a few days off, which would make his wife happy. Fishermen kept long hours that could stretch into days or even weeks, and she often accused him of loving the sea and his boat more than he did her. In a funny sort of way, he wasn't so sure that she was wrong. In spite of the cold and the dark and the inherent, ever-present danger – one crab fisherman a week died during some seasons – crab fishing was in his blood; and in the summer, he missed it.

But he wasn't getting any younger and the cold was starting to seep into his bones and linger in a way that hadn't happened when he was a younger man. They said it took its toll on you eventually. The ocean claimed you one way or another; you couldn't cheat it forever. But maybe he could be the exception. Maybe, with enough catches like this one, he would be able to retire early. Move away from the icy grip of Alaska to somewhere down south, somewhere hot. Then his wife would smile at him again like she did when they were younger and want him in her bed if he didn't smell of crab all the time.

He was kidding himself maybe, but it was a pleasant enough fantasy.

He whistled to himself as he sorted through the crabs, pleased to see a few good-size red king crabs, or Kamchatkas as the natives called them: big, almost dangerous looking creatures that could achieve a leg span of nearly three feet. Nightmare looking pincers on them that could do a lot of damage if you weren't careful.

As well as the red kings there was a good stash of golden and blue, which weren't as heavily prized as the reds but still commercially viable. There were a few of the smaller scarlet crabs as well, which he would take home to his wife to be frozen for the coming months.

Raul was still whistling when he spotted something unusual.

Something that made the tune die in his throat.

It was sticking up through the mass of crabs. It was pale, brown, and fleshy looking, far too soft and the wrong color for a crab leg. As he hauled it closer, he saw the raw, bloody stump at the end and the myriad network of bites going up it. Even before the rest of it surfaced, he felt a growing horror and a scream rising up in his chest.

It was a body.

If you could even call it that, it was so badly eaten away. The crabs' last meal had been an extravagant one.

As the long dark hair came into view, the only part that Raul could see that the crabs had left untouched, a long, guttural moan came from between his dry lips. His hands were clammy, and he could feel himself breaking into a cold sweat that covered every inch of his skin. He should put it back, he told himself, and call the police. Let them lift it out. This was too much for him. Yet he continued to haul the body towards him even as the dread of what he was about to see bubbled up in him.

Don't look at the face; don't look at the face.

But as the body came closer, it turned of its own accord, and almost against his will he found that his gaze was drawn to what was once the woman's face, now only a mess of tissue and bone.

Finally, he screamed.

CHAPTER TWO

Her father slammed the door shut so loudly that Special Agent Sadie Price visibly flinched against the noise.

Sadie had been expecting this reaction. It was one of the many reasons that she had been determined, on her arrival back in Alaska, that she would do her best to ensure that her path never crossed her father's. Sadie expected nothing else but rejection from the old man. The mean old bastard had been rejecting her for her whole life.

Sadie hadn't come here for a heartfelt family reunion. She had come here to get some answers about her sister's death. Her sister's murder.

But it was more than just her bitter disappointment about not getting answers that made her eyes sting with sudden tears. She wiped them away furiously with the back of a gloved hand, telling herself that it was just the cold making her eyes water, nothing more.

Snow fell softly around her. The storm had let up, but the radio had promised it was a brief reprieve. Sadie pushed her scarf down and inhaled deeply, feeling the subzero air threatening to freeze her lungs, but almost welcoming the stab of pain. It was nothing compared to the stabbing in her heart. Why had she ever thought that he wouldn't be able to get to her anymore?

It was nearly Christmas but there was no sign of lights or decorations at her father's cabin. He was a recluse these days, she had heard: a lonely, bitter old alcoholic. His wife dead of cancer, his favorite daughter murdered, and his other daughter estranged. No chance of happy families here. Sadie and her father were estranged for good reason.

She could remember other Christmases, when she had prayed for her father to ignore her just as hard as she had prayed for him to love her.

*

"Dad. Don't! She didn't mean it," Jessica pleaded as their father rounded on Sadie, his shotgun in his hand as he grabbed it from above the fireplace. It wouldn't be the first time that he had trained it on her, to scare her or try and subdue her into submission. The first time, Sadie had still been in junior high, and she had wet herself as her father turned it on her, just inches from her face.

That had been just a few weeks after Mom had died.

"He doesn't mean it," Jessica had whispered to her that night as she had cuddled a sobbing Sadie to sleep in the dark of their bedroom, torn between loyalty to her father and her younger sister. Just a child, Sadie had known even back then that it was a lie. He did mean it. She had no doubt that if her father could have gotten away with it, then he would have pulled the trigger on his youngest daughter. The one that he had never wanted, as he often took great pleasure in reminding her.

She was surprised that he hadn't done it already. Suddenly, thirteen-year-old Sadie didn't care anymore.

"What I said is true," she said, her angry eyes fixed on her father. "Mom would have left you if she had lived, and you know it. She hated you just like I do. You make us all miserable."

"Sadie, stop," Jessica pleaded. As their father stepped forward, the gun in his hand lined up perfectly with the center of her forehead, Sadie wondered if he was finally going to do it. The hatred in his eyes was palpable.

Then Jessica stepped between them. "Please, Dad," she said softly. "It's Christmas."

His eyes went from one sister to the other, and slowly, he put the gun down. He wouldn't hurt Jessica. Then he grabbed for his coat and made his way to the door without saying a word to either of them. Before he left, he kicked the forlorn little branch of pine that they had decorated and stuck in a pot, in lieu of a proper tree. The small presents that Jessica had bought with her meager wages from her Saturday job at the hardware store had gone, sold by their father for more booze money. It had been the heartbroken look on Jessica's face that had prompted the argument between Sadie and her dad.

They both let out a sigh of relief as the door slammed shut behind him. This time of year, he could be gone for a few days.

"I managed to get hold of some chicken bones to make stock," Jessica said. "So, we can have broth and potatoes. And I got party hats. It will be just like a proper Christmas dinner," she said desperately, trying to salvage some festivity. Sadie nodded.

"Yeah, it will," she said, forcing a smile. She watched Jessica go into the tiny kitchen.

"Merry Christmas," Sadie said to no one in particular.

*

Sadie forced the memory away and set her shoulders back as she prepared to knock on the door again. She wasn't thirteen anymore and had stopped being scared of her father long before she had left town to go to college. Until a few days ago, she hadn't been back since. Apart from the occasional birthday card, which he had never reciprocated, there had been no contact. She had always been happy for it to stay that way.

But things had changed. Her father had stage four cancer, for one. On its own though, Sadie wasn't sure that would have been reason enough to get her outside his door. Instead, it had been the words of a different dying man.

What happened to my sister?

Ask your father.

Implying that he knew something, after all these years, and had never said a word. That he had done it? She couldn't, wouldn't believe that, but in the dead of night with nothing else to distract her, it had always been the possibility that played on her mind. Her father had loved Jessica – at least, as much as he was capable of loving anyone, but he hadn't been above raising his hand even to his favorite daughter.

Sadie had always suspected that her father was secretly relieved when the case had been dropped. Her sister's body, bloated and frozen from being trapped under the frozen lakes, hadn't yielded any clues as to how it had gotten there. Without any other evidence, it had been ruled inconclusive. Case closed.

Sadie had known better. Her sister had been murdered. And now she had been told that the person who could answer her questions was none other than their less than doting father.

She would drag the answers out of him if she had to. Jessica's murder had haunted her for years and it was one of the reasons that she had returned to Alaska. Unfinished business. Because, although Jessica's death had been investigated after her body had turned up following her mysterious disappearance, no conclusions had been made. It could have been an accident. It could even, God forbid, have been a suicide. Or so the locals had whispered, not looking Sadie or her father in the eye. Ice both bloated and preserved bodies, making both exact time and cause of death impossible. The case had been dropped.

Sadie had known, deep in her gut, that someone had killed Jessica; but who wanted to listen to a wayward fifteen-year-old with a chip on her shoulder?

She was a hotshot BAU agent now, renowned for having caught some of the nation's most sinister killers. If there was anything to find out about her sister's death, she would find it, and this time people would have to listen to her.

There were other reasons for leaving Washington, D.C., as well, but she wasn't going to think about them right now. One past trauma at a time, she thought wryly.

Sadie was about to bang on the door again and let her father know that she wasn't going anywhere until he answered it and answered her, when she heard her radio crackle.

It was Sheriff Cooper, who was just a few hundred yards back on the track and waiting for her in the snowplow along with Deputy Jane Cooper, his sister.

"I'm sorry Price, but I need you to get back here," he said. There was a tone to his voice that made the hairs on the back of her neck stand up in both fear and anticipation. It was a tone that she had heard too many times over her career not to recognize.

Something had happened.

"What is it?"

"A body has been found down at the harbor, in a fisherman's hold. It doesn't look good. We need to go and check it out," Cooper sounded apologetic, but urgent.

"I'll be right there," she told him.

Sadie turned and made her way back to the snowplow without glancing back at her father's cabin.

She would be back. But right now, it looked as though she had another, more recent murder on her hands.

CHAPTER THREE

Sadie stepped onto the boat, holding her breath against the smell and clenching her stomach against the nauseous roiling of the waters. Even in the harbor, the waters were choppy after the storm had been raging over Anchorage and the surrounding areas for the last few days. Seawater lapped up the side of the dock and the air tasted of salt.

She looked around for the fisherman that had found the body, noticing the state of the boat. It was one of the smaller ships, and its machinery was old and looked in need of repair. A lot of the crab fishermen, she knew, needed to keep expenses down and so there were too many boats in the water that were frankly dangerous. If a ship went down completely once it was out at sea, the Coast Guard frequently couldn't get to it on time to prevent fatalities.

Crab fishing was a dangerous game, and so the fishermen themselves tended to be resilient folk, not easily spooked.

The man who crouched near the hold in front of her, however, looked like a broken man. He looked up as Sadie and the Coopers approached, and Sadie saw the recent horror in his eyes. Whatever he had seen down in the hold, Sadie knew, was going to give him nightmares for the rest of his life.

"I've been doing this since I was a kid," he said as the Sheriff introduced them. The fisherman's name was Raul. "I've been around the crabs all my life. Seen some right big 'uns. I know some people find them frightening, but me, I love 'em. Tasty critters they are. People will pay for good Alaskan crab meat." His expression twisted and Sadie thought he was about to cry. "Never knew they could do that to a body though. Like something out of a horror film."

Sadie crouched down next to him, trying not to think too hard about what he had just said. "You must have had an awful shock," she said softly. "But you have done the right thing by calling us straight in. Is the body still in the hold?"

The fisherman nodded, staring at Sadie with haunted eyes. "I threw a sheet over it. You will have to go in there and see for yourselves. I'm not going near it again."

"That's okay," Sadie reassured him. She stood up and glanced at Jane who was hovering over them. No one was in a rush to go into that hold and see what had terrified Raul so badly.

"Deputy, do you want to take this man's details while the Sheriff and I go and check out the body?"

Sadie half expected Jane Cooper to look annoyed at Sadie taking charge, but instead the other woman looked relieved and nodded.

"Sure," the other woman said, giving her a grateful smile. Sadie took a deep breath and followed the Sheriff down into the hold.

"I don't think this going to be pretty, Cooper," Sadie said in a low voice as they approached the figure in the corner, haphazardly covered by the sheet. A lock of long dark hair showed at one end and, at the other, a lump of flesh that might once have been a foot.

The Sheriff didn't say anything, but even in the dim glow of his flashlight Sadie could see that he already looked nauseous. As the local Sheriff, dealing with both Anchorage and the surrounding hinterlands, he wouldn't have seen too many bodies. Accidents, mostly, a few domestics and suicides, but nothing like the things that Sadie had seen, and even she was wishing that she didn't have to look at what awaited them under that sheet.

Cooper lifted the sheet carefully, mindful not to disturb anything. The ME had already been called out and forensics were on their way, although the snow would slow them down. Resources were scarce out here, and Anchorage often had to share with neighboring cities.

Sadie held her breath, against both the mingled smell of shellfish and death, and to steady herself against whatever she was about to see.

It was only a quick glimpse, partly obscured in the gloom of the hold, before Cooper dropped the sheet and spun around, retching, but it was enough. Sadie closed her eyes against the nausea that filled her. She could taste the bile in her throat, but she held it down.

"Okay," she said, breathing slowly. "That was pretty bad. We are going to have trouble identifying her – assuming it is a her."

"It was a her," Cooper said, sounding wretched as he wiped his mouth. "I saw...I saw...it was all eaten away."

He retched again and this time he threw up, but thankfully far enough away from the body not to contaminate it. Sadie averted her eyes. Sometimes, it happened. Cops were only human, and Sadie had seen hardened homicide detectives suddenly throw their guts after years on the job. She would never mention it to Cooper; she would pretend that she had never seen it.

Even so, the Sheriff straightened up and glared at her accusatorily, as though it was her fault he had vomited. He was just embarrassed, she knew, but she felt a little stung. After a hostile start, they had begun to work well together on their last case, and it pained Sadie that he thought that she would react to his momentary weakness in any other way than with compassion.

Mind you, he had recently seen her break a grown man's nose.

She turned around and made her way back to the ladder. "Let's go and see what the fisherman has to say," she said neutrally.

As she came back up onto deck she took large breaths of the harbor air, which tasted of crab and salt and snow. The Deputy looked over at them, took one look at her brother's face and grimaced.

"That bad?" she said sympathetically.

"It might be hard to identify the body," Sadie said, still carefully not looking at the Sheriff.

"This is Raul," Jane told her, nodding at the fisherman. "He found the body just before he called it in, while he was clearing out the hold. Says it has no idea how it got there."

Sadie noticed that Raul's hands were trembling. "Of course. Were you the only one on board, Raul?"

He nodded, opened his mouth to speak and then shut it again. He was in shock, Sadie thought, and no wonder.

The Deputy answered for him.

"He told me there are usually three of them, but the other two had gone home because of the storm. They didn't want to get stuck aboard the ship for Christmas. But Raul wanted to check out the rest of the catch, because it was a good one. That's about right isn't it, Raul?"

Raul nodded again, although Sadie wondered if he had really heard anything that the Deputy had said. He looked dazed. He pulled a packet of cigarettes from out of his pocket and lit one with shaking fingers. The wind and wet air meant that it took a few tries to get it to stay lit. They stepped away from him, giving him some privacy. The Sheriff was standing at the side of the boat, looking out across the harbor, scanning the other ships.

"I took the names of the other men on board," Jane said, "But there are people all over the harbor, all times of day and night. Anyone could have taken an opportunity to put the victim in the hold. We will need to interview anyone who has been here over the past few days."

As Sadie agreed, Cooper turned around, frowning.

"We don't know yet that anyone did put her there," he cautioned. "Let's not jump to conclusions yet. We need to establish that this is even a murder before we start talking about victims."

The Deputy shrugged, unfazed. "Just thinking ahead," she said. "It's a bit of a weird place for a body to turn up, right? Can't say as I've ever heard of it before."

Sadie agreed with Jane. It was possible, of course, that the body had been picked up with the catch rather than been placed directly in the hold, but even if that was the case, there was the question of how the body had gotten into the sea in the first place.

She shook her head, hardly able to believe that this was happening right off the back of solving a serious murder case. They had been on their way to the Coopers for shelter from the storm and a well-deserved rest, and now it looked like they would be getting neither.

Sadie had expected Alaska to be quiet, at least compared to her previous posts. Instead, the action hadn't stopped since she had arrived.

It was almost as though she had brought trouble with her.

"I agree," she said, looking out over the harbor. It looked almost pretty under the moonlight. "We should do a search. Check the rest of the holds."

Cooper's eyes swiveled around to her in horror, and Sadie guessed that his thoughts hadn't gone straight to the possibility of having to see any more bodies that were in the state of the one below.

"On the evidence of just one body," he said impatiently. "We don't even know how it got there. You can't order a full search of the harbor because of one body in one hold. It would take hours and cause uproar among the guys. This is the height of crab season, and these men need to be out on the water doing their jobs. A search could take all day or even longer. And likely turn up nothing."

"We don't know anything yet; I'm with you on that," Sadie agreed. "But then wouldn't it be better to err on the side of caution? If this is a murder, then there could be others. And better the bodies are found by professionals than any other fishermen. That isn't going to do them much good either, is it? I'm pretty sure he's going to need a few days off after this."

She glanced over at Raul who was now leaning over the side of the boat at the opposite end, still looking shell-shocked. A few days off was probably an understatement.

"Why would there be any others?" Cooper snapped. Sadie raised her eyebrows at his tone, surprised and annoyed by it. "Even if this is a murder that we are looking at here, not every murder is a serial," he said, softening his tone as he continued. "You've done a great job on this last case, and we couldn't have solved it without you, but don't you think that you might be letting it cloud your judgment? It was you who was warning me not to jump to conclusions, before all this."

Sadie eyed him, saw the strain on his face and the shadows under his eyes, and shrugged. He was making a valid point and maybe she could be overreacting. Neither of them – nor Jane, who had ended up in the hospital too – had had time to process recent events. Part of her wanted to chew him out for the way that he had just spoken to her, but she exhaled slowly and let it go.

"Okay," she said, "we'll play it your way, Sheriff. Let's wait to see what the ME has to say about the cause of death, and we'll go from there."

She decided not to add that if there was even a hint of a suspicion of foul play, then she was giving the order to search the holds. As local Sheriff, this was Logan Cooper's jurisdiction, but as a Fed, she could override him on this, a fact of which she knew he was aware and no doubt resented.

Sadie had no wish to play pissing contests; it wasn't her style. But back in D.C. she had a reputation for her instincts always being on the nose, and right now they were screaming at her.

Screaming that this body was only going to be the first.

CHAPTER FOUR

Sadie felt like screaming as she looked down at the body on the slab in front of Pete, the local Medical Examiner. Like most MEs that she had met, he had a clinical, stoic air about him, and was so used to seeing the dead that it was humdrum to him. Just another day at the office.

When Sadie had seen him inspect other bodies, the examiner had been respectful but detached, not seeming personally fazed in the slightest. And living in Alaska, he no doubt would have seen bodies that had been killed by animals before. Bears, mostly.

But even Pete looked sick to his stomach at this one.

This body was something else. There was a thudding in her ears as she tried to focus on what Pete was saying, and she knew that she would be seeing this sight in her mind's eye for a long time. She carefully avoided looking at the Sheriff, hoping that he wouldn't vomit again, for his own pride.

Jane had taken one look when Pete had pulled the sheet back and then excused herself. Sadie and the Sheriff unfortunately had no other option but to bear witness.

"The left hand, as you can see, is virtually gone," Pete said, nodding at the pulpy mess, "and the right side, all of the fingers have been nibbled away."

"No fingertips then," Sadie concluded with a sigh. It always seemed wrong to her when a body had no known identity. Because a body was never just a body. It was – or at least had been – a person, with a name and a family and a life. A history and a personality. A story. Without that they were nothing but a metaphorically faceless victim.

This one didn't even have a face. No metaphors about it.

"Afraid not," Pete responded. "We'll have to wait for the lab results for her DNA. And of course, that will only help if she's in the system. No missing persons, I presume?"

"No," Sadie said, "although communications have been down because of the storm." She glanced at Logan Cooper to see if he knew more, but the Sheriff had his lips pressed tight together. His skin was deathly pale under the lights of the station basement, and he had a stiff set to his shoulders as though he was concentrating solely on holding himself together. She looked away.

"I did get something very interesting from the preliminary bloodwork though," Pete said, holding up a test strip.

Sadie peered at it, noticing the positive result on one of the segments. "She was on drugs?"

"Benzodiazepines," Pete confirmed. "And way more than would have been on her prescription, assuming that she even had one."

Sadie blinked as she took this latest bit of information in, her mind whirring with the possibilities. She could have deliberately overdosed, prescription pills being one of the most popular ways for females to try and kill themselves, but that didn't explain how she had gotten into the hold, or why she had removed her clothes.

Overdosed and then stripped off and jumped into the ocean, only to get caught up in a fishing catch? That didn't seem right to Sadie. It meant too many coincidences, and in her experience, coincidences were usually anything but.

But the other, more horrific and, to Sadie's mind, more likely possibility didn't bear thinking about. She closed her eyes and spoke very slowly, as though doing so could guard against the intrusive images that now filled her inner eye like her own personal horror movie.

"She was sedated," she said slowly. "And then thrown into the hold?"

The ME nodded grimly.

"I'm afraid it looks that way. Ruling out sexual assault – which so far there is no sign of – it would also explain her nakedness. Less for the crabs to get through. Of course," he cautioned, "With the body so eaten away, it's completely possible that I'm missing something, but at this stage my conclusion is that the cause of death was indeed the crabs themselves. Death by a thousand cuts, so to speak."

"A thousand pincers," Sadie said hollowly and without humor. Next to her, the Sheriff made an audible gulping sound.

"But she was sedated?" she said, as a creeping horror filled her. The thought of it, being trapped in the hold, while hundreds of crabs crawled over her, pulling away her flesh little by little…Sadie couldn't imagine a worse death, and she had seen some horrific things.

Pete met her eyes for the first time over the body and she could see her own horror reflected in his gaze, although his voice was as professional as always, calm and measured as he went about his job. Sadie suspected that Raul wouldn't be the only one who couldn't sleep tonight.

"She would have been out of it for a long time with that level of benzos in her bloodstream," he said, and Sadie breathed a sigh of relief only to snatch it back as he continued.

"However, we don't know how much time elapsed between her being given – or taking – the drugs and her being placed in the hold. It would have taken a long time for her to die. Hours. She could have come round in that time. In fact," he paused, and Sadie had the childish urge to stick her fingers in her ears so that she couldn't hear any more.

"Go on," Cooper said in a strangled voice. It was the first time that he had spoken.

"Some of these bite marks on the underside of her arms," Pete said, lifting an arm so they could see what he meant, "the pattern looks as though she was trying to defend herself. So it's possible -even probable -that she was awake for at least some of it."

"My God," Cooper breathed. He turned around, facing the wall and taking long, deep breaths. Sadie rubbed a hand over her forehead. It was freezing down here but she suddenly felt uncomfortably warm and dizzy, as though she might pass out at any minute.

"I think it might be a good idea to take a quick break, Pete, for us to get some air?" she suggested. Pete shrugged.

"You two go ahead. I prefer to just get straight on with these things, you know?"

Sadie nodded at him and climbed the stairs back into the station house, Cooper close behind her. She went straight for the back door and opened it, sucking in the cold and, for once, welcoming it.

Would it have been as icy in the hold, she wondered, packed to the rafters with all those crabs, all climbing and crawling over one another?

She shook her head fiercely. *Don't think about it*, she told herself sternly. The only way to cope with these things was to get on with the case. Seek justice. That was her job. She couldn't change what had already happened, but she could do something about it.

The thought helped, turning the horror to anger. Whoever had done this to the poor woman, she swore to herself that she would get the bastard.

"Thanks," Cooper said suddenly, startling her out of her thoughts. He was next to her, staring up at the sky. His tone was surly, though, rather than grateful. Sadie frowned.

"Thanks for what, exactly?"

"Getting me out of there," he said shortly, and Sadie understood the surliness. He thought that she had felt sorry for him and made an excuse to get him out of the basement before he threw up again.

"I was getting myself out of there, Cooper," she said honestly. "I needed some air, or I was going to pass out."

He looked at her and she could see the relief in his eyes.

"Really? I thought you were coping pretty well. I was…well, you saw. In the hold." He looked up again and she saw the humiliation on his face.

"Logan," she said, using his first name for perhaps the first time since she had met him, "it happens to all of us, sooner or later. It's nothing to be embarrassed about. I'm telling you, five more minutes and I would have fainted or been sick myself. Even Pete is struggling. The state of that body, and knowing what caused it…," she shuddered, unable to complete the sentence.

"It was her face," he confided. "Or lack of, anyway."

She nodded, understanding. Facial injuries were the worst. It was more than the gore and the sheer grotesqueness of appearance; there was something dehumanizing about them that only amplified the horror.

"So, you've been sick at a body before?" he went on. She could hear the desperate need for reassurance in his voice and knew that this wasn't just a 'man thing' but a cop thing, too. He needed to know that he wasn't the only one who had chucked his guts up on the job.

Sadie nodded. "My first child case was a particularly brutal murder." She shivered at the memory. "I threw up all over the morgue floor, and my superior slid in it on his way out."

Cooper looked horrified at the thought. "Did they…?"

"Mock me?" she finished for him. "No. Oh, maybe some teasing happens with a rookie if it's a fairly standard body, not that anything is exactly standard in our line of work. But not with kids; they get to the toughest of us, and definitely not with what came out of that hold. Quite frankly, I'm surprised we haven't gone stark, raving mad."

Cooper gave her a relieved smile, and then he squared his shoulders, the tough Sheriff again. "Shall we go back down?"

"Yeah, let's get this over with," she said with a sigh, hoping that Pete wasn't going to discover any more gruesome details.

As they descended the stairs and approached the body, Pete was staring into the mouth, frowning, and Sadie felt an awful sinking feeling in her stomach that her hopes were going to be dashed. The ME looked up as they stood on the other side of the unknown victim and waited for him to speak.

"I think we can definitively say that this was a murder," he said. Sadie knew that Medical Examiners rarely made pronouncements like that. There was always room for error.

"What have you found?" Cooper asked. He sounded back in control and his voice was sharp.

"The tongue has been taken," Pete pronounced. He pried the mouth open to show them, but Sadie didn't look. She was more than happy to take Pete's word for it.

"But surely that was the crabs as well?" Sadie said. After all, they had made a feast of the woman's eyes and the cartilage on her nose and ears.

"Unfortunately – or perhaps not, depending on how you want to look at it – it wasn't. The incision is too clean. It was done very carefully, almost surgically."

"By the killer," the Sheriff said. A statement, not a question. His eyes met Sadie's and she knew that he was waiting for her to confirm his thoughts. After all, this was her area of expertise.

"A trophy," she said flatly. Killers, particularly of the serial and psychopathic variety, tended to like keeping trophies. It wasn't always a body part of course; it could be an item of clothing or piece of jewelry, but it would always be something personal. Something to remember their victims by, and to remind them of their own prowess and the joy of the kill. It was sick, and it was also a pretty good predictor of what they were potentially dealing with here.

A serial killer.

"Sheriff," she said, "we need to search those holds."

CHAPTER FIVE

Sadie watched carefully as the two men in front of her cleared out the hold, mumbling under their breath the whole time. As Cooper had predicted, they hadn't been too happy at giving up valuable fishing time, especially as the reasons given had been vague. Sadie knew that they needed details about the body kept out of the press for as long as possible.

Deputy and Sheriff Cooper were on other boats, but even with them taking a hold each, they would be lucky to be done by nightfall. Cooper had pulled a few State Troopers off their usual shift to assist, but the weather conditions meant that no one was traveling too far out.

Sadie hadn't been back to the Field Office in the center of Anchorage since the day she had arrived. She had spent the night before at the Coopers, slipping into a mercifully dreamless sleep, too exhausted for even the horrors of the crab eaten body to make it through her slumber.

"There's nothing here," one of the fishermen said, swinging his flashlight. So far, they had been a surly lot, some of them deliberately dragging their feet, showing their annoyance at what they clearly felt was a waste of their time and effort.

"Could you check under that tarp there?" Sadie asked, trying not to show her impatience. As the day wore on and nothing was turning up, she was feeling more and more agitated. The thought of any more women being trapped in with a pile of crabs made her skin crawl. They couldn't afford to drag their heels.

The man rolled his eyes but did as he was asked, pulling the tarp up and shaking it out, carefully shining the flashlight into every inch of the hold that had been uncovered. He looked at Sadie with raised eyebrows.

"Nothing there, ma'am," he said.

"Thank you," Sadie said and climbed up onto the deck, ready to start on the next boat.

As she approached it, the harbormaster walked over to her. A tall, thin guy in his mid-thirties, he had a world-weary expression and thinning, sandy hair.

"Is this going to take much longer, Agent?" he said. "I wouldn't expect you to know, but we are at peak crab fishing season here. This could lose the guys a big haul."

"Actually, I'm a local," Sadie countered. "And we're sorry about the interruption, but this wouldn't be happening if it wasn't of immediate importance, Mr…?"

"Robert Holmes," he said. "Rob is fine. Only my mother calls me Robert." He gave Sadie a smile that made him look suddenly much more handsome, and Sadie was reminded of just how long it had been since she had a date. Her job didn't allow her much time for love, not that she was one to go looking for it in any case.

There was no mistaking the appreciative look in the harbormaster's eyes however as he smiled at her. His gaze managed to take her in from head to toe without making it obvious that he was checking her out. Sadie was suddenly acutely aware of her messy hair and the fact that she was bundled up in more layers than a bag lady. For an Alaskan, she had always been way too sensitive to the cold.

"Deputy Cooper wasn't very forthcoming with the details," he said, obviously hoping to get more out of Sadie. "Although she did ask me a lot of questions about my own movements over the past few days, and whether I had seen anything suspicious."

"And have you?" Sadie asked. Handsome smile or not, there was something slimy about Robert Holmes that made her immediately wary of him.

"Nothing, I'm afraid," he said, still smiling. "I try and run a tight ship here." He laughed at his own joke. Sadie ignored it and scanned the harbor.

"How many people would you say are here on any one day?" she asked. The harbormaster looked thoughtful.

"At the height of the season? Hundreds, easily. The commercial fleets can be up to eighty boats, and there are at least twenty independents. Each will have a small crew. Then you've got the dockhands. It's seasonal laboring work, of course, so they tend to come and go. Dockhand work isn't always official, if you know what I mean?"

Sadie raised an eyebrow. "Shouldn't you keep an eye on that? Illegal workers can lead to modern-day slavery issues, you know. The fishing trade is notorious for it. Then there's people smuggling. I'm sure you don't need me to tell you the kinds of things that could go on here."

The harbormaster looked offended. "I oversee everything as best I can," he said. "We don't want anything like that here. I just meant that it's precarious work for the dockhands. It can be hard to keep track of who is working where."

"I appreciate that," Sadie said. "If you do think of anything unusual, please do let us know," she said with a polite smile before she started to walk away.

"It was a body you found, wasn't it?" the harbormaster said, his voice low and confidential. "I was called in to watch the harbor while forensics were here."

He was eager to talk about it, Sadie could tell. Which was perhaps normal enough, but she couldn't help wondering if it wasn't due to the narcissistic need killers often have to be close to the investigation. Making a mental note to check out his background, she smiled tightly and left him, in order to board the next boat and resume the search.

There was nothing on that one, either.

Or the one after that.

*

The harbor was silent again.

Sadie stared through the front window of the snowplow, watching a cloudy moon illuminate the waters below it. The search had taken all day and it had been getting dark before everyone else had finally gone home, leaving her and the Sheriff to wait behind, in the hope that their search would have kicked up enough fuss to worry the killer into coming back to cover up his tracks.

"It's quite common for killers like this to return to the scene of the crime even without a practical reason," Sadie said, her eyes sweeping the harbor now for any sign of movement.

Cooper shook his head. "That makes no sense," he protested. "Why would they be that stupid?"

Sadie shrugged. Her years in the Behavioral Analysis Unit had taught her that people's reasons for doing things were often incomprehensible to outsiders. Sometimes there were no reasons.

"Serial killers – assuming that's what we've got here – are usually very clever in certain ways, but never as clever as they think they are.

There's often a sense of entitlement and narcissism that makes them want to be known, to assert their power over us ordinary folks, and that means stupid mistakes. They want to glorify in their memories of the kill – it's euphoric for them, maybe linked to a sense of revenge or mission – hence the trophies and the returning."

Next to her, she felt Cooper shudder.

"Whatever is going on in this guy's mind, it's gotta be pretty depraved to dream up this type of death," he said, the disgust evident in his voice. "I mean, he must have known the body would be found, that the crabs wouldn't be able to consume it all. They're not pigs."

"He knew," Sadie nodded. "The horror was deliberate. If it was about somewhere to discard the body, the victim would have been killed first. The sedation must have been so he could subdue and transport her, not to ease her pain. He wanted her to suffer."

"Do you think the tongue is symbolic of anything?" Cooper asked, and Sadie was glad that he trusted her expertise enough to ask her questions. Their first day working together had been fraught, to say the least.

"Trophies usually are," she confirmed. "Especially with body parts. A tongue seems obvious – it's about silencing. It's never a good idea to assume though, because symbols can be subjective. Tongues might mean something to our killer that's very personal to either him or the victim."

"It would help if we knew who she was," Cooper said, sighing heavily. "It makes it so much harder to know anything with no victim identity."

Sadie sighed with him and then wiped the interior side window so she could better watch the side of the harbor. Sitting around like this made her feel impatient. She knew it was necessary – often a bigger part of policing than people realized – but she preferred to be in the middle of the action, or leading analysis, rather than just waiting to see if something was going to happen.

"I hate just waiting around like this," Cooper said. Sadie laughed lightly.

"You read my mind."

"How about we use the time so you can tell me a bit more about yourself?" he suggested. Sadie felt herself stiffen. He already knew that Sadie was a local and he knew about Jessica. That was enough personal detail, she felt. During ten years as a Fed down South, she had never spoken about her past to anyone.

"What is there to know?" she said defensively. Cooper shrugged, although she saw the spark of interest in his eyes at her reaction and cursed herself. Now he would just be even more intrigued.

"You had a great career down South," he said. "It seems odd that you gave it all up to come back to Alaska. I know you have questions about your sister's death that might have brought you back, but why now, after all this time?"

Sadie fought the urge to tell him to mind his own business. Her superior back at Anchorage Field Station, Special Agent Golightly, had asked her much the same thing, but she could hardly blame people for wondering. It did seem odd. It *was* odd.

"There was a difficult case," she said slowly. "It made me question things, I guess, about where my life was going and who I was. And that meant thinking about the past, and all the unfinished business that I have up here. I ran away from it, all those years ago. I never returned until now."

"A lot of people do run away," Cooper said, sympathy in his voice. "Alaska tends to be one of those places. Especially when you're from the hinterlands rather than the town. There's not many opportunities for a young person with any sense of ambition."

"Sure," she agreed. "I was always going to go to college out of state. But after Jessica died, then it became about running away."

There was a silence, during which all she could hear was the wind outside and the spattering of snowdrops on the front of the plow. Cooper cleared his throat.

"Isn't that what you're doing now? Running away from whatever happened back in D.C.?"

Sadie didn't reply. Her cheeks burned, although whether that was with anger at him questioning her or humiliation because she knew that he was right, she couldn't have said. Sheriff Cooper was too damn astute for his own good.

"I'm sorry," Cooper said when the silence stretched on. "I shouldn't have said that."

"No," Sadie said flatly, "you shouldn't. I'm here to do a job, and my reasons for leaving D.C. don't affect that."

There was an awkward silence and Sadie felt bad for her tone, but she didn't appreciate Cooper digging around in her business. Another reason Alaska had seemed an attractive destination after D.C. was the fact it was far enough away that gossip was unlikely to reach.

"You can ask me questions instead if you want," Cooper offered. "I'm pretty much an open book. Not that I'm implying you're not," he finished hurriedly, then groaned. "I'm making a real mess here, aren't I?"

Sadie couldn't help laughing. "It's alright, Sheriff. I don't need to know your secrets," she teased, glad that the tension had passed. Then she asked in a more serious tone, hesitating slightly, "There is one thing, although it's not really about you...have you ever looked into the case on my sister? Ever...heard anything?"

Cooper looked at her, frowning, and was about to reply when Sadie caught a glimpse of something from the corner of her eye. A flashlight.

"Look," she hissed, "there's someone getting on that boat, over there."

Cooper followed her line of sight, and they saw a guy boarding a boat further down the harbor. Sadie couldn't make out his features, but he was wearing yellow rain gear that made him immediately noticeable. They watched him move across the boat, and then the flashlight went out.

"Let's go," Sadie said, unclipping her seatbelt. They got out of the snowplow, careful not to make too much noise. Sadie was holding her breath, her hand reaching instinctively for her gun. Could they have found the killer already?

"Wait," Cooper hissed. "The flashlight's back on, he's getting off."

"He was fetching something," Sadie guessed.

They watched the yellow clad figure disappear into a small shack at the opposite end of the harbor.

"He's gone into the Bait Shack," Cooper said, heading towards it.

Sadie drew her gun and followed.

CHAPTER SIX

Sadie wrinkled her nose against the pungent smell of the Bait Shack as they stepped inside. The man had turned on a dim lamp, which gave off a dirty yellow light that pervaded the gloom with the color of stale urine.

"Who are you?" The guy in the rain gear jumped near enough out of his skin as Sadie and Sheriff Cooper entered. He was coming towards them through an interior door that led to another, smaller room, and he had a look on his face that Sadie recognized as guilt. When the Sheriff and Sadie flashed their badges, his right eye twitched alarmingly. Still, he seemed to be no immediate threat, and Sadie slid her gun back into her holster.

Being trigger-happy had gotten her into trouble before.

"Sheriff Cooper, and this is Special Agent Price. Is there a reason you're here at this time of night?" Cooper asked.

The man seemed to flinch at Cooper's words, but he raised his chin stubbornly. He was an average sized, middle-aged guy with stubble and strands of greasy salt-and-pepper hair escaping from under a woolen hat. Broken blood vessels on a slightly bulbous nose suggested that he was a heavy drinker.

"This is my shack," he retorted stubbornly. "I'm Joe Higgins. I source and sell bait for the guys, and help out on the boats sometimes too," he said proudly, as though it was the greatest achievement of his life. Perhaps it was. Sadie could have felt sorry for him, but there was something unsavory about Joe Higgins that made her not want to get too close.

But was he the killer?

"We saw you go onto one of the boats and then come into here," Sadie said. "It looked as though you were fetching something, is that right?"

Joe's eyes went wide and scrabbled around the room, as though looking for an answer in its dark corners. It was as clear as day that he was hiding something.

"No," he said quickly. Too quickly. "I was…checking that you guys had tidied up properly. I've heard that you can leave an awful mess when you do searches. No respect for the public, some would say."

Cooper looked almost amused as he raised an eyebrow and pointedly looked around the Bait Shack, which was hardly evidence of a preoccupation with cleanliness. "It seems a little late to be cleaning up, Mr. Higgins. You're going to have to do a bit better than that. What were you really doing on the boat?"

Higgins shook his head stubbornly. "I already told you," he said. He sounded angry, and underneath that, Sadie could hear a note of panic in his voice. Sadie's noticed his eyes flicker towards a corner of the room, towards a stand where a variety of cutting tools, from knives to cleavers, hung. Her hand went back to her holster. Just in case.

"You have," Cooper agreed amiably, "But I'm afraid we don't believe you. Why would you decide to come out at this time of night and decide to 'check that we hadn't made a mess,' as you put it? Surely you can see that doesn't sound very likely."

"I've got OCD," the man said. "So, I get obsessions with things. I got it into my head that the boat was a mess and there was no way I could get back to sleep until I had checked. Okay?"

Sadie and the Sheriff exchanged glances. That sounded plausible, but Sadie was willing to bet her last dollar that the man was lying. He was hiding something, probably in the back room that he had been coming out of when they had entered the shack. They couldn't search it without a warrant, which meant they were wasting time.

Sadie looked at Cooper and jerked her eyes towards the back room, hoping he would understand her. If the Sheriff could keep Higgins talking then Sadie might get the chance to look around in there.

"That sounds terrible, Mr. Higgins," Cooper said to the man politely. "And we certainly don't want to cause you any more distress. I might just need to check that, however. Do you have the name of the doctor who diagnosed you?"

Higgins looked affronted. "You can't speak to my doctor!" he yelled, his voice suddenly rising. "That is an invasion of my privacy!"

"It would just help if you could give us a few details, that's all," Cooper said soothingly. Higgins looked at the floor, his temper seeming to fade as quickly as it had come, and while the Sheriff was keeping the man occupied Sadie slipped through the small doorway into the back room and looked around.

There was little to see, other than trays of labelled, pre-prepared bait and a pile of tattered fishing magazines with titles like 'Alaskan Fisherman' and 'Crab Catcher.' But there could easily be something hidden in the bait boxes. Squinting against the dim light and peering into dark corners, she looked around for any alcoves or ledges on the walls, while at the same time listening to the conversation coming from the other room.

"Well, I haven't actually been diagnosed," Higgins was mumbling. "I don't trust doctors. Big Pharma, they're all just corrupt, trying to poison us with drugs."

"I see," Cooper replied, and Sadie grinned to herself as she heard in his voice the urge to roll his eyes at the man. "So that means you can't corroborate your story. That leaves us in a bit of a bind, Mr. Higgins."

"I shouldn't need to prove anything!" Higgins yelled suddenly. The guy seemed more than a little unhinged, his sudden displays of temper at odds with his overall expression. "I haven't done anything wrong! You have no right to come in here and question me like this!"

"The thing is," Cooper continued, sounding unfazed by the other man's agitation, which would no doubt agitate him even more, "We do need to know what you were doing on that boat. Because I reckon maybe you left something on there, something that you managed to keep out of the way of the searchers earlier today, but now you're worried in case we come back. So, you decided to move it to somewhere a bit safer."

"That's nonsense!" Higgins all but screamed. Hearing the desperation in his voice and remembering those rows of knives, Sadie walked back towards the other room. The back of her neck was tingling: a sensation that she always associated with the premonition of danger.

Cooper still sounded calm, and Sadie could see him now; he was framed in the doorway, his posture relaxed. Only another cop would notice how his right hand was casually draped over his belt near his holster, and his feet in a position that would make it easy to pivot in an instant.

"Get out!" Higgins yelled, his face red with fury. There was spittle coming out of the corners of his mouth. As Sadie stepped through the doorway, he swung around to face her, his expression contorted.

"What are you doing back there? I didn't say you could snoop around!" he accused.

“Just having a look,” Sadie said calmly. “You have a good stash of bait in there.”

The man flinched as though he had been stung. “You keep away from my things,” he said desperately.

“If you haven’t got anything to hide,” Sadie said reasonably, “then it wouldn’t hurt to let us have a look around, would it?”

Higgins blinked at her, momentarily lost for a comeback. He was volatile, Sadie thought, and apt to go off at any moment.

“Otherwise,” Cooper added, “we are going to have to get a warrant, and you wouldn’t want us making a mess in here, would you? Not with your OCD.”

His comment seemed to tip the man over the edge. Moving faster than Sadie would have expected such a heavyset man to be capable of, Higgins snatched the largest cleaver from the rack of tools and charged at Cooper before there was any chance of the Sheriff drawing his weapon. Higgins swung the cleaver at the Sheriff’s midriff, just as Sadie rushed in, her gun pointing straight at Higgins.

“Drop the weapon!” she screamed.

Everything seemed to be happening in slow motion. She saw the blood spread across Cooper’s jacket and saw him stagger backwards, and her finger tightened on the trigger, ready to shoot Higgins. To kill. It was justifiable defense – he had attacked a fellow officer with a cleaver. Sadie had been taught how to react in these situations, and protecting Cooper, not sparing Higgins, was the priority.

Then Higgins saw her and saw the gun. He hesitated, wavering, and then dropped the cleaver, crumpling into a ball on the floor with his hands raised above his head.

Sadie’s finger was still squeezing.

“Don’t shoot!” Higgins sobbed, his anger gone as quickly as it had escalated.

There was a roaring in Sadie’s ears and her heart was pounding in her chest. For a split second, she thought it would be too late, but then she lowered her gun and slipped it back into the holster before stepping forward and grabbing Higgins. She pushed him, roughly, face down to the floor and cuffed his hands behind his back, ignoring his protests that she was hurting his arms. Then she grabbed her radio and ran over to Cooper at the same time, crouching down next to him with her heart in her mouth.

Don’t die on me, Cooper, she thought, dreading what she might see.

He was groaning in pain and clutching his hands to his stomach. Blood pumped through his fingers, spreading rapidly over his torso. He looked up at Sadie, his blue eyes burning with agony in his now pale face.

It didn't look good. In fact, it looked very, very bad. Sadie radioed through for help, clutching Cooper's hand as she did so, willing him to be all right.

Willing him not to die on her.

CHAPTER SEVEN

Sadie tried not to wince as she watched the nurse stitching Cooper up. The wound, despite the copious bleeding, had thankfully turned out to be superficial. Nothing serious; but it was bloody, and it was going to be sore. Sadie had breathed a sigh of relief when she had realized that the Sheriff wasn't going to expire on her after all, feeling faintly guilty even though she knew that without her intervention Higgins could have done a lot more damage before Cooper had managed to draw his weapon.

This was the second time in just a few days that she and Cooper had ended up in the ER. The nurse that was stitching him up, a pretty redhead who kept giving the Sheriff admiring glances as he sat there with his shirt off, pursed her lips disapprovingly every time she looked at Sadie. As though his repeated visits were somehow her fault. Or perhaps she just resented the presence of another woman. For reasons that Sadie didn't want to examine, the nurse's obvious liking for the Sheriff was riling her.

"I do recommend you stay in the hospital until the morning, Sheriff," the nurse cooed. "You need to give your stitches a chance to settle. Hopefully they won't scar too noticeably." Her eyes ran over his torso, making it clear what a shame it would be to ruin the tanned skin and rippling abdomen that Sadie was deliberately not looking at. Hadn't even noticed in fact, she told herself firmly.

"Not a chance of that," Cooper said matter-of-factly. "We have an interrogation to be getting on with."

"I can take care of that," Sadie offered. "The Deputy can take your place. I'm sure you'll be in good hands here," she said with only the faintest touch of sarcasm. The redhead bristled and Cooper looked amused.

"I'm sure I would be," he agreed, and the nurse smiled at him adoringly in a way that made Sadie want to vomit. "But I want to be there. It was me he tried to chop up, so I want the privilege of nailing the bastard."

"I can't argue with that," Sadie said. "You're lucky it's only a flesh wound; that cleaver was sharp."

"I'm not sure about lucky," Cooper said, tipping his head to one side as he looked at Sadie. "I seem to have been really unlucky since you turned up. It had been quiet for months, and now wham! All the criminals seem to be crawling out of the woodwork at once. You're like some kind of psychopath magnet."

He laughed to show that it was a joke and Sadie mustered a smile, but she didn't find it very funny as she felt that stab of guilt again and superstitiously wondered if there wasn't some truth to Cooper's words. They had barely had a chance to breathe since she had arrived in Alaska; it was almost as though she had brought some kind of curse in her wake.

"All done, Sheriff," the nurse said, her voice cutting through Sadie's morbid thoughts. She taped a bandage around Cooper's side and Sadie was sure that her hands lingered on his body in a way that wasn't wholly professional, her nails lightly grazing his skin.

"I'll let the doctor know that you want to go Sheriff, and he'll come and check that you're fit for discharge." The nurse walked off, not even bothering to acknowledge Sadie. There was an exaggerated sway to her hips and Cooper watched her go.

"She was nice," Cooper said, grinning. Sadie raised an eyebrow.

"Nice? She was practically drooling into your wound."

Cooper grinned at her. "Jealous?"

Sadie eyed him coolly until Cooper coughed and looked away.

"If we could get back to the case," Sadie said stiffly, hoping that her cheeks hadn't gone red, "What do you think of Higgins as our perp?"

Cooper frowned. "It seems fairly obvious, doesn't it? He was trying to cover his tracks in some way, and I doubt he went at me with a cleaver just because he didn't like my tone."

Sadie didn't answer but sat staring out of the window. The foggy sky was clearing, and the snowfall had stopped. She would be able to go back to the motel that she was checked into once they were done. It was unlike her, but she wasn't relishing the thought of being alone tonight. The incident with Higgins had scared her, and not just because of the way she had felt when she had thought that Cooper might have been seriously harmed.

It was just how close that she had come to shooting Higgins, and to killing him. It had been instinctive, with no thought process to speak of. *Her first instinct had been to kill him.* She shuddered, and the gun in her holster suddenly felt heavy, resting on her hip like a reminder of the responsibility that she always carried. She became a cop to help people, not kill them; but sometimes the world just wasn't that simple.

She had learned that the hard way.

"Are you okay?" Cooper asked her. He looked at her with genuine concern, even warmth, and Sadie felt oddly vulnerable.

She didn't like feeling that way.

Vulnerable was what got people hurt.

"I'm just not sure about Higgins," she told Cooper, neatly sidestepping his question. "You're right; it seems obvious, but I can't help thinking there's something else going on here. We need to know what it was that he was bringing off that boat."

Cooper nodded, agreeing with her. "We can't jump to any conclusions until we've questioned him. If this doctor doesn't hurry up, I'm going to discharge myself."

Sadie didn't argue with him, knowing that she would do exactly the same thing. Higgins was their biggest lead after wasting a day on a fruitless search, and whether he was the killer or not, they had clearly stumbled across something.

"It does seem likely that he was hiding evidence though," Cooper went on. "Something that we had managed to miss during the search. The syringe that he sedated her with, or something else that could have the victim's DNA on it. The tongue, maybe?"

"He will have kept the tongue close. Also, it was a different boat," Sadie pointed out. "How likely is it that he would have her on one boat with a perfectly good crab hold, and then transfer her to another? Unless he was trying to frame Raul or one of his shipmates. We can't rule them out, either. Although Raul would have to be an Oscar winner to fake that reaction yesterday."

"Jane questioned them all, and there's nothing to go on," Cooper said with a sigh. "But maybe they were all in it? If we could get an ID on the victim, we might be able to discover what links her to the guys at the harbor. There has to be something, right?"

Sadie pulled a face as an image of the body flashed into her mind. To kill someone in such a horrific way…it felt personal. The outcome of a burning hatred and desire to hurt. The killer either knew his victim, or she symbolized something that was important to him. Something that he detested.

"There's always something," Sadie agreed. "Even if she wasn't personally known to the killer, he obviously came into contact with her, and this doesn't feel opportunistic. But without an ID there is so little to go on. Perhaps Higgins can enlighten us…he strikes me as someone who will talk easily now that he doesn't have a shack full of weapons. You have some leverage over him too now…he could be looking at an attempted murder charge." She jerked her head towards his bandage.

The Sheriff still hadn't put a shirt on, and Sadie shifted uncomfortably, still carefully avoiding looking at his brown skin and tight pecs with the dusting of dark hair between them.

"If I ever get out of here," Cooper grumbled impatiently, "we might get the chance to find out."

"We've been here less than an hour," Sadie said, looking at the clock on the wall. "They have already rushed you through."

"There are some perks to being a Sheriff," Cooper said wryly.

"Like pretty nurses?" Sadie quipped, and then wished that she could take her words back. It was meant to be a joke, but it came out sounding catty as hell, and Cooper just gave her that grin again. Sadie swiveled around in her seat so that she was no longer looking at him.

They sat in silence for a moment, Sadie staring at a poster on the wall that was warning elderly patients about the signs of pneumonia, not wanting Cooper to see that her cheeks had flamed in embarrassment. What the hell was wrong with her? She had seen a half-naked man before.

Okay, so it had been a while.

"We can search the Bait Shack now that Higgins is in custody," she said eventually, addressing the poster. "If he was hiding something then it had to be in the back room, maybe among the bait boxes. There were trays and trays of them. Why don't I go and do that while you're waiting for the doctor?"

She was already on her feet before Cooper even had the chance to agree. She needed to be doing something, taking action, not sitting around feeling awkward, trying not to think of too many things that were swirling around in her mind.

"That makes sense," Cooper said, although she thought she caught a note of disappointment in his voice, and Sadie wondered if that was because he wanted to be there for the search or because she wasn't staying with him. She suspected that he didn't like hospitals any more than she did. "It will give him more leverage when we question him."

"That depends on what I find," Sadie said as she put her jacket on. She remembered the missing tongue.

She left without looking at the still half-naked Sheriff.

*

Back at the harbor, Sadie made her way carefully towards the Bait Shack. At this time of night, no-one was around, and she could only see a few lights in the distance across the water, from a few boats that were still out. Independent fishermen, most likely, struggling to make a living as the commercial fleets took over.

The smell of salt, crab, and fish seemed even stronger, somehow, than it had during the day and Sadie wondered if it would ever properly wash out of her clothes. She badly wanted a hot shower.

It was a shame that nothing was ever going to wash the memory of seeing that body away.

As she entered the Bait Shack another smell hit her nostrils. Blood. Spilled on the floor from where Higgins had lunged at the Sheriff with his cleaver. She remembered the desperation and panic in the bait man's eyes, behind his defensive anger. Because he was about to be caught for murder?

Or something else?

Inside the Shack, Sadie shone her flashlight into the back room and went straight in there, heading towards the bait trays. She took them out one by one, wrinkling her nose as she pulled on gloves and started carefully sifting through boxes of fresh diced meat, herrings, clams, and turkey necks.

There were a lot of boxes, and she moved swiftly and methodically, making her way through the stacks of trays. Finally, she picked up a box that felt slightly heavier than the others. With her heart thumping, she placed the box carefully on the floor and lifted the lid.

A pile of turkey necks, densely packed, stared up at her. Sadie started to carefully remove them, and then uncovered a folder and, next to it, a wad of cash. She lifted the folder and laid it on the floor. It was a simple, A4 binder that anyone might find in an office, and she opened it, wondering what it was she had discovered. Illegal gambling among the fishermen, maybe, or a list of people acquiring stolen goods? Drugs crossed her mind, although that sort of operation would usually be a lot more efficient than this.

Instead, what she saw in the folder made her recoil in horror, dropping it as though it had burned her hands.

It contained nude photos, a whole selection of them, clearly of the amateur variety. But it wasn't your typical, run of the mill pornography.

The subjects of the photographs were children.

Her hands shaking, Sadie pulled out her phone to ring Cooper.

"I've seen the doctor," he said immediately on answering. "Just waiting for the discharge letter."

"You might not want to bother," she said. Her voice sounded faraway, as though none of this was quite real and she guessed that she was in minor shock. Of all the potentially horrific things that she could have found, she hadn't been expecting this.

"You've found something," Cooper said, immediately alert. "What is it?"

Sadie told him. She heard the Sheriff's shocked intake of breath, and when he spoke, his voice was hard in a way that she hadn't heard before.

"I'm coming now," he said. "I'll meet you at the station."

Sadie walked back to the snowplow, holding the folder as though it was a bomb that was about to go off, her lip curled in disgust as she thought about Higgins.

She wondered if she should have pulled the trigger after all.

CHAPTER EIGHT

Sadie arrived at the station to find Cooper already there, sitting opposite Higgins in the small interrogation room. He had pulled up his shirt to reveal the bandage, casually inspecting the wound in front of its creator.

"It looks worse than it is, I'll grant you that," Cooper was saying to the man as though he was chatting to an old acquaintance. "But any deeper and I could have been a dead man. You narrowly missed some vital organs there, Joe. Is that what you were after, becoming a cop killer? A tough prison sentence that would be. You'd get a lot of hassle from the guards. Still, it might not be much better for an attempted cop killing, you know? The inmates might just think you were a pussy that couldn't get the job done properly."

Higgins sat opposite him, hunched in his chair and with his beady eyes fixed on Cooper. They were burning with resentment. In spite of his surly demeanor, he couldn't quite manage to hide the fear in his expression at the Sheriff's words.

"You're just trying to scare me," he said sulkily, but with a slight tremor in his voice. He looked up as Sadie came in.

"He'll get even more of a rough time inside," Sadie said, not bothering to try and hide her disgust as she met Higgins's eyes, "If we show them these pictures. Child abusers don't do well in prison."

Higgins's look changed to one of sheer terror as Sadie raised the folder in her hand. "That's not mine!" he protested, looking around him wildly.

"What are you looking around for Joe, another cleaver?" Cooper asked him. "You won't find anything to help you in here. You would be better off co-operating with us. You're in a lot of trouble. That's before we even get started on the murder investigation."

"I haven't done anything!" Higgins yelled. "That's not even mine. It's got nothing to do with me," he said as Sadie sat down next to Cooper and placed the folder on the table in front of her.

"Then how do you know what it is?" Sadie asked. Higgins blinked rapidly, his eyes darting between Sadie and Cooper. Then he slumped in his seat, looking defeated. His hands were chained to the chair. "I'm not saying anything," he mumbled. "Police harassment; that's what this is. I could sue."

Sadie ignored him and opened the folder, carefully fanning out the photographs so that Higgins could see them. Beside her, she felt Cooper stiffen.

"I need a quick word outside, Agent Price," he said quietly. Sadie looked at him in surprise, but quickly nodded and followed him outside, gathering up the photos.

In the hallway outside the interrogation room, Cooper leaned against the wall, letting out a slow exhale. Sadie waited for him to speak, knowing exactly how he felt. No one wanted to deal with this. She would rather see a hundred crab eaten bodies than contemplate what could be happening to those kids.

"This night is going from bad to worse," Cooper said in a strangled voice. "I'm not sure how I'm going to get through this without ripping that guy apart."

"I know," Sadie said softly. "But we've got him. He's going to prison one way or the other after his stunt tonight."

"Too good for him," Cooper snarled. He looked at Sadie and there was a haunted look in his eyes.

"I recognized some of those kids," he said in a strangled voice. "They're from around here. Local families."

Sadie felt the contents of her stomach roil like the waves in the harbor. She pressed the back of her hand to her mouth. "What the hell is going on here?" she said through her fingers. "The parents...are they..."

"They're good people," Cooper finished for her. "I can't believe that they would know anything about this."

Sadie didn't want to tell him that all too often, in these cases, it was a family member who was the primary abuser. The Sheriff would already know that, but it was always a tough thing to contemplate if you knew the people involved. It was one of the reasons Sadie had always been glad to be a Federal Agent, working a long way from home, rather than a local cop. Some things were too close for comfort.

"I'll have to inform Golightly about this," Sadie said, referring to her superior at the Alaska FBI Field Office. A potential child pornography ring was likely to be an interstate matter...pluck one string of a pedophile web and it too often turned out to be bigger than anyone could have predicted.

"Let's see what we find out first," Cooper said. "It could just be a local ring. Higgins doesn't strike me as much of an organized crime maestro...I mean, photos and wads of cash in the harbor?" He shook his head in disgust. "We need to know where he's getting those pictures from. Whether or not he's the one taking them."

Cooper looked as overwhelmed as he did angry, and Sadie empathized with him, wondering if it was the first time that he had dealt with anything of this magnitude. Child abuse was all too often hushed up, often for years, even in this day and age.

"Does he have any priors?" Sadie asked.

"He's not on an active register, but I'll go and check the database. Do you want to come with me, or do you want to see if Higgins will be more receptive to you on your own?"

Pleased that he trusted her to handle the suspect by herself, Sadie nodded. There was often antipathy and rivalry between the local cops and the Feds, with the locals seeing the federal forces as riding roughshod over their jurisdictions, and some agents dismissing locals as provincial hicks. Both the Coopers had distrusted her on her arrival, so the Sheriff treating her as a colleague meant a lot.

"I'll concentrate on asking him about the body in the crab hold first," she said, "and we can discuss the photos when you get back. If you know the families, you're more likely to know the right questions to ask."

Cooper nodded at her and walked down the corridor. Sadie watched him go; then she took a deep breath and headed back into the room to Higgins.

He was laid back in his chair, his arms crossed, and his head tipped back, staring at the ceiling. He sat up as Sadie walked back in, looking at her warily. Forcing a polite smile, Sadie sat down.

"I don't think the Sheriff is very happy with you," she said, inspecting her nails casually. Higgins glared at her.

"I know how this goes," he said. "I've seen the primetime shows. You're just trying to make me scared and make me open up to you, right? Well, it won't work," he said smugly, clearly impressed with his own cleverness. "I know all about psychology; I do. Took an evening class."

"You must be a very clever man. Have you thought of university?" Sadie asked sweetly, looking up from her nails. "No," Higgins said sulkily. "That costs money. Selling bait doesn't bring in too much money these days."

"Ah, I see. I guess that's why you turned to selling pictures of naked kids, is it?"

Higgins didn't answer but just looked down at his shoes. Sadie stared at him for a few moments, letting the tension build in the room. Then she said softly, as easily as though they were simply discussing the weather, "Why did you kill her, Joe? And why like that?"

Higgins nearly jumped out of his chair, his eyes wide and startled. "I didn't kill nobody!" he screamed. Sadie noted the difference in his reaction to when she had asked him about the photos and wondered if he was telling the truth, or just panicking at realizing exactly how much shit he was in.

"Did she have something to do with the photos?" Sadie persisted. "Perhaps she found out and was threatening to turn you in? You couldn't have that, could you? So maybe you decided the only thing you could do was to silence her?" Sadie thought again about the missing tongue.

Higgins looked as though he was going to cry. "I didn't do anything to anybody," he said stubbornly. "You're bullying me, that's what this is."

"No-one is trying to bully you, Joe," Sadie said reasonably. "You're under arrest, and the Sheriff and I have a job to do. Namely, finding out why you are sedating women and throwing them into crab holds. That another sick fetish of yours? Crabs?"

Higgins looked like he was going to be sick. "That's disgusting. You're disgusting," he complained.

"More disgusting than taking naked pictures of children?"

Higgins closed his eyes. "I didn't take them," he said.

"Then who did, Joe?" Sheriff Cooper asked as he came back into the room and took his seat again next to Sadie. He rested his forearms on the table and looked at Higgins with a carefully blank expression even though Sadie guessed the Sheriff would like nothing more than to break the man's jaw, at the very least.

"I don't know," Higgins said obstinately.

"You would be better off cooperating, Joe," Sadie told him. "Because you're really not in a great position here. We have you dead to rights on assaulting the Sheriff here and on possession of pornography of children. Distribution too, judging by that wad of cash I found next to the pictures. On top of that you're under suspicion for murder. If you actually took the pictures, that's even worse. If you can give us a name on the other hand...well, it always looks good in court if you're cooperative."

Sadie knew that no amount of cooperation was likely to help him if he was responsible for putting that woman in the crab hold, but Higgins may not know that, and daytime TV wasn't exactly known for its accuracy.

"Those girls are local, aren't they, Joe?" the Sheriff said through tight lips. "How do you know them? They're not fishermen's kids. How were you coming into contact with them?"

Higgins shook his head. "I don't know them," he said. "I didn't take the pictures."

"So, you were just selling them? For who?"

Higgins looked at his feet again. He looked defeated now, and Sadie wondered if he was about to confess. Instead, he just repeated, "I want a lawyer," and then leaned back and closed his eyes.

Sadie and the Sheriff exchanged glances. They couldn't keep questioning him without a lawyer present when he was asking for one, or it could prejudice the case. Cooper sighed.

"Well," he said, yawning, "I guess that means myself and Agent Price here can go to bed. There won't be any lawyer here until the morning at the earliest. Perhaps longer with the way the roads are right now. Enjoy the cells." He stood up, and Sadie followed him. As they made their way to the door, the Sheriff looked back at the man sitting at the table.

"I found your file from Juneau," he said, and Higgins eyes flew open again.

"That was a long time ago!" he protested.

Cooper shrugged. "It seems old habits die hard," he said. "It just looks worse and worse for you, doesn't it? Goodnight, Joe."

Outside the room, Sadie looked at Cooper. "Okay, what did he do in Juneau?" she asked.

"Exposed himself to some kids on the way back from school," the Sheriff said. "It was ten years ago. He escaped prison, due to his lawyer pleading he had depression and anxiety. He had therapy instead. His sheet has been clean ever since...which probably just means he hasn't been caught."

Sadie pulled a face. "The therapy clearly didn't work, huh? I'm not sure how to make sense of all this."

"We have to tell the parents and speak to the kids," Cooper said, looking pained. "I'll get Jane on it in the morning; she's great with kids. What do you think about him being our killer? Did you discover anything?"

Sadie shook her head, feeling frustrated. "No, he flat out denied knowing anything about it. And to be honest, my first reaction was to believe him. He reacted very differently to our questions about the pictures. I suspect we're looking at two different cases, but..."

"But?" Cooper asked.

"Well, how much of a coincidence can it be? Just how much is going on down at that harbor?"

Cooper rubbed his face with his hand and Sadie saw how exhausted he looked.

"I can't think about all of this right now," he admitted. "I'm about to fall asleep on my feet. Let's pick up again with Higgins in the morning when he has a lawyer present, and we can see what Jane can find out from the parents."

"Okay," Sadie agreed. "I had better go back to the motel now that the storm is over, or that sour-face landlady will be renting the room out. I'll take the truck."

Cooper walked her out of the station, raising a hand in goodbye. "Get some sleep," he told her, although Sadie thought that, out of both of them, he was the one who desperately needed it.

As for her, she needed a drink.

But first, she wanted to take another look at that boat.

CHAPTER NINE

As he drove down the deserted dirt road, a heavy fog descended over the road. It made him smile. He liked the fog. There was something eerie about it.

And it made it easier not to be seen.

He kept his eyes out for the café that she had mentioned, feeling his mouth going dry in anticipation. He hoped that she looked just like her picture; you could never tell over the internet these days, not with all the fancy filters and things that women could use. Making themselves look like cartoons. He preferred the natural look.

He didn't like being lied to either; and it was a form of lying, the way they made themselves out to be someone else online. Of course, he could be accused of doing the same. He smiled to himself again. He hadn't actually lied to her though, had he? Just omitted a few details.

Like, why he really wanted to meet her. And what it was about her that had initially attracted him to her profile. She didn't need to know those things, not yet.

By the time she did realize, it would be too late.

His hands were clammy on the wheel as he drove slowly, anticipation leaping in his belly as he saw a small shack appear out of the fog with a wooden sign hanging on it that said 'Café' in bright red painted letters. It was closed now of course. There was no one around.

Except her, standing in front of the café and looking around her. She saw his car and smiled, stepping forward. Silly girl, he thought. He could be anyone.

He was pleased to see that she was just as pretty as her picture had showed her to be. Prettier, in the flesh. Her long dark hair fluttered around her face in the wind, and she was wearing black boots, a woolen navy coat and matching scarf. She looked neat and demure. Not too much makeup either. He hated it when women made themselves look like whores.

He pulled over and wound down his window, which crackled with frost. He could see his breath in the air. He called the name she had given him, and she came over to the car. Straight to the passenger side, ready to get in. It amazed him how dumb some of these girls could be. Didn't they ever read the news? Maybe things were different where she came from.

She was certainly more demure than American girls. Polite and not flashy. As he drove away, she waited for him to speak, and seemed genuinely interested in what he had to say. Not like the brash girls you got here, who didn't know their place.

It was all an act though; he wasn't so stupid as to not know that. She was being as dishonest as he was. Trying to reel him in for money or a green card.

They were all the same, in the end.

"How are you finding it here?" he asked her, not really caring. Still, he needed to keep the pretense up until he could keep her quiet.

"It's very nice," she told him in broken English. "People are very nice here."

"That's good," he took his eyes off her for a moment and then smiled at her, putting at her ease. The fact that she had no idea what was about to happen to her excited him. Her wide, oh-so-innocent eyes looked at him under her long lashes. She was probably eyeing up his wallet, he thought.

"So, do you enjoy your job?" he asked. She nodded and started to tell him more about it.

This was when he started to get irritated, when they gabbed on about their stupid lives. Making out like they were so sweet and caring, such nice girls. That was the real lie, the part that mattered.

She wouldn't be lying anymore, not after tonight. He would make sure of it.

"How about you?" she asked, and for a moment he couldn't remember what he had told her about himself, and it threw him of course.

"I'll ask the questions," he snapped, and he saw her shrink back, startled by his tone.

"I'm sorry," she said, casting her eyes downward. "I did not mean to offend."

She was submissive and apologetic. It should have appeased him, but instead he just felt a white-hot anger boiling up inside of him, followed swiftly by the familiar desire for revenge. For justice. He hit the gas, turning off the main track and taking her on smaller paths that only a local would know.

"Not far now," he said. The atmosphere in the car was tense now and he could see her looking out of the window and sense her sudden realization that she was alone in the backwoods with a guy she didn't know, who suddenly didn't seem so friendly. He inhaled deeply, as though he could smell her fear.

It excited him.

"Where are we going?" she asked timidly.

"You'll see soon," he told her. "We're nearly there." She didn't seem soothed. In fact, he saw her hand fluttering by the door handle as though she was contemplating throwing herself out of the car.

He sped up. "It's locked," he told her, not bothering to pretend anymore.

"I…I need to go back," she stammered. "I left something."

He ignored her and drove on. She seemed to give up, sitting back in her seat, but he could feel the tension coming off her and her hands were so tight around the handle of her purse that her knuckles were white.

Soon, he would give her something to relax her.

Permanently.

"Where are we going?" she asked again after a while. It was completely dark outside now.

"Don't worry," he said. "It's just five minutes away and we will be there. I have a *very* special place picked out for you."

CHAPTER TEN

The harbor was still quiet, although Sadie could see that a new boat had docked and there were a few figures moving around on board. A couple of dockhands were moving equipment around, their head lamps lighting their way. Compared to the daytime, however, the place was as good as deserted.

As Sadie walked past the two dockhands, she saw them notice her, looking her up and down and then grinning at each other.

"Are you lost, sweet cheeks?" one of them said, openly leering. The other had a small scar over his right eye, shaped like a crescent moon. The beam from the flashlight highlighted it, making it look like a tattoo.

Sadie stopped in front of them, smiling and then whipping out her badge.

"Actually, no," she said, suppressing a grin of her own as the leer quickly disappeared. The man who had addressed her looked horrified while the other burst out into laughter, shaking his head at his now thoroughly embarrassed colleague. Sadie walked on, her eyes on the boat up ahead, where she and Cooper had seen Higgins fetching his stash of pictures.

There were a few things that were bothering her about that, hence her decision to check the harbor one more time. Namely, how the day's search had failed to turn up the photographs. As well as the holds, equipment lockers had been checked. There had to be a hiding place, and in that case, what else might be there?

There was still the question of that tongue…not to mention the syringe that must have been used to sedate the victim. If they could find something to tie Higgins to the body as well as the photographs they might actually get somewhere. Although her initial impression was that Higgins himself wasn't the killer, she could be wrong.

Sadie almost hoped that she was wrong, because that meant that they had the killer in custody, where he couldn't hurt anyone else.

So, another look couldn't hurt.

It could have waited until the morning, when she could bring the Sheriff with her, but if Sadie was honest with herself, she was also avoiding going back to the motel, and not just because it was rundown and cold. She had been having nightmares ever since her return to Alaska and after the day's events it seemed a safe bet that it wouldn't be long before her next one. If she exhausted herself enough, then hopefully she would sleep deeply enough to not be awoken by night terrors. Last night, at the Coopers', she had experienced the best sleep since the first night that she had arrived here.

Part of her had wanted to stay there, in a real home, in a comfortable bed, with an actual family. Although she only knew them professionally, the Cooper siblings seemed close.

She missed that.

Sadie made her way up onto the boat, the *Blue Betty*, and started to look around, wondering what they could have missed. She lifted up nets and ran her hands along the sides of the boat but turned up nothing.

She made her way onto the bridge and then dropped down onto the lower deck, crouching down to inspect and feel underneath a pile of ropes in the corner, even while knowing that this had all been checked.

There had to be *something*.

Then, she heard footsteps on the harbor, approaching the boat.

Switching off her light, she crouched down by the nets, waiting, hoping the leering dockhand hadn't decided to follow her.

Sadie heard the footsteps board the boat, moving purposefully overhead. Whoever it was knew where they were going. Keeping down, she slid up onto the bridge, lying flat, and saw a man walking across the upper deck.

A fisherman that she vaguely recognized from the searches earlier that day, a small guy with a stutter and a bad case of acne, was heading towards the equipment lockers, a large flashlight in his hand that illuminated half of the deck. Sadie pressed herself backwards, further into the shadows.

She watched as he reached the equipment lockers and reached underneath one of the lower ones, feeling around for something and shining his light directly on it. Sadie couldn't make out what he was doing until there was an audible click and a thin tray slid out.

A secret compartment. She cursed to herself silently. If all of the lockers had those, then they would have to search them all over again.

The fisherman swore to himself, shining the flashlight closer to the tray, which of course was empty. Sadie straightened up and stepped out into the light.

"Looking for something?"

The man nearly jumped out of his skin. He whirled around, raising his flashlight as though to shield off a blow. When he saw Sadie, he lowered it and then put both of his hands up.

"Pl…please don't sh…shoot," he stammered, looking as though he was about to cry.

"I'm not going to shoot you," Sadie said impatiently. "Well, not unless you try anything."

"I…I won't," he promised. He seemed oddly childlike, and Sadie wondered if there was a developmental issue at play. She tried to put her revulsion at the content of the pictures he had been looking for to one side, telling herself to go easy on him if she wanted to find out anything useful.

"I just need to ask you a few questions," Sadie said. "And hopefully we can keep you from getting into too much trouble. What's your name?"

"Johnny," he said, blinking through tears. "My m…m…mom is going to be m…mad."

Sadie couldn't help but feel sorry for him, although she would reserve judgment until she got the full story.

"Were you looking for pictures, Johnny?" she asked, carefully keeping her voice neutral. "Pictures of little girls with no clothes on?"

Johnny's face crumpled. "He s…s…said it was okay because the g... girls weren't being hurt. I just c…collect the money and give it to him. But I s..s.. said they were only l... little girls. H... he s…said he would tell my mo…mom if I didn't."

As she pieced together what Johnny was telling her, Sadie felt even more disgust towards Joe Higgins.

"Let me check I've got this right, Johnny," she said slowly. "Someone was getting you to distribute those pictures for him? He was paying you?"

Johnny shook his head rapidly. "N…not paying m…me!"

Sadie pressed a hand to her forehead to relieve the aching that was rapidly growing in her nerves.

"Why were you doing it then Johnny? You must know it's wrong, right? You said it yourself; these are just little girls. And this is hurting them. Little girls shouldn't be made to take their clothes off for pictures, Johnny, you know that don't you?"

Johnny nodded, looking shamefaced. Sadie gave him a moment to reply, not wanting to push too hard as the guy looked on the verge of collapse. He was young, she saw in the beam of the flashlight, no more than nineteen, but mentally he was clearly a lot younger.

"H…he said he w…would tell the c... captain that they were my pictures and I w…would lose my j…job and go to p... p... prison," he stammered, his eyes wide with fear at the memory. Sadie felt a hand ball into a fist at her side. She believed the kid, and in that moment wanted nothing more than five minutes on her own with Higgins.

"Who said that, Johnny? Joe Higgins?"

Johnny looked shocked. "H... how did you kn…know?"

"Because he is currently in a cell down at the station," Sadie told him. "We found the pictures that you were looking for in his Bait Shack. We know that they're his. He's in a lot of trouble Johnny…and you might be too, unless you tell me what you know."

She kept her voice soft, not wanting to sound as though she was threatening him, but Johnny started to tremble with fear, nevertheless.

"I c... can't g…go to p…prison," he said, his stammer getting worse as he started to panic. "It w…would k…kill my m…mom."

"That's not going to happen, Johnny," Sadie told him, "As long as you're telling me the truth. You are telling me the truth, aren't you?"

Johnny bobbed his head up and down rapidly, while Sadie thought about her options. He had admitted distributing the pictures, but it was clearly under coercion and threat, which meant Higgins was the perp here, not Johnny. Arresting the kid and throwing him in a cell overnight would be cruel. But she needed to know what else he knew.

"Where was Higgins getting the pictures from, Johnny?" she asked. "Who was taking them? Was it him?"

Johnny looked confused, as though the question had never occurred to him. Perhaps it hadn't. The kid had most likely just done as he was told, too scared of Higgins's threats to think any further than that.

"Okay. So, who were you selling them to?"

That was the one thing that didn't make sense to Sadie. Why bother with Johnny, who clearly wasn't very bright, as a middleman, when Higgins had plenty of access to the harbor and the fishermen himself? Unless it was just a way to try and keep his own hands clean, leaving Johnny in the frame. He was obviously scared of the bait man.

Now, knowing that Higgins had already been caught, Johnny would no doubt sing like a canary in a coal mine. If she could get the boy to make a formal statement, they would hopefully have a lot more leverage over Higgins, encouraging him to talk too. There had to be more to this than just a few pictures, as bad as they were. Who was getting access to these kids, and what else was being distributed? In this day and age, pedophiles gathered and swapped their filth online. There couldn't be much money in just selling a few pictures to fishermen.

But how did all this connect to the body in the hold? Was there even a link?

"S... some of the f…fishermen," Johnny said. "H…Higgins t…told me not to s…say they came from h…him."

Sadie shook her head, briefly closing her eyes. So, she was right, Higgins was using the kid as a foil. So, they now had him for the pictures and for taking advantage of a vulnerable person.

What a lowlife.

"C... can I g... go now?" Johnny asked, looking hopeful. Sadie sighed and shook her head.

"I'm afraid not, Johnny. What you've told me is very, very serious. You have admitted giving out the pictures, which could get you into a lot of trouble. If you hadn't told me about Higgins threatening you, then you would be in a cell right now."

Johnny was now crying, a long dribble of snot hanging down from one nostril. Sadie tried not to notice.

"W... will I g... go to par…prison?" he asked, looking terrified.

"Not if you co-operate," Sadie said, thinking fast. She didn't want to bother Cooper right now, knowing the Sheriff needed to get some rest after his run in with Higgins and his cleaver, but she had to play this carefully. Johnny's statement would be crucial.

"I tell you what Johnny," she said after a few moments punctuated by Johnny blowing his nose on his cuff, "I'm going to take you home and talk to your mom, okay? I can release you into her care tonight as long as you promise to come to the station first thing in the morning and make a statement about everything you have told me. Then I can keep you out of trouble."

Johnny wiped his eyes. "My mo... mom will be m…mad at me," he said. Sadie wondered who he was more scared of, his mother or Higgins.

"It's either that or I have to take you to the cells," Sadie said, wincing when Johnny let out a high-pitched wail of horror before nodding his assent and letting Sadie lead him off the boat and towards the snow truck.

She looked up at the sky, which was clearer now, a bright moon riding high above the inky waters of the harbor and sighed deeply. She should have been pleased that she had found what could be a breakthrough with Higgins, but instead she just felt desperately sad for Johnny, the girls in the photos, and the unknown woman in the hold. On nights like this, the world seemed like a dark, cruel place.

As she shut Johnny in the truck, Sadie checked the watch on her wrist, wondering if the saloon would still be open.

She might just have time for that drink after all.

CHAPTER ELEVEN

Sadie walked up to the bar, sliding onto one of the stools, grateful to find the saloon still open past midnight. Thinking about it, Sadie hadn't yet known the saloon to be shut. Winter in Alaska meant night fishermen, trappers, and hunters. Many of whom needed a stiff drink now and then, just like Sadie did right now.

Caz, the bar owner, looked surprised to see her. She was a broad woman, with short red hair and tattoos, who, in spite of her tough appearance, had a warm air about her. Sadie liked her.

"A double Scotch, when you're ready Caz," Sadie asked her. Caz raised a pierced eyebrow.

"I think it's the first time I've seen you off duty, Agent," she said. "Bad day?"

"You have no idea," Sadie murmured. She felt exhausted and all her limbs were heavy with the need to sink into a deep sleep. At the same time, she was buzzing with nervous energy, her mind racing.

She hoped the Scotch would help. It had been some time since she'd had a drink, and she needed something to take the edge off after the day she just had.

Johnny's mother had been predictably horrified to find out what had been going on, and Sadie had no doubt that she would be frog marching her son up to the station first thing in the morning. The detective in her was looking forward to questioning Higgins again on the back of Johnny's statement. `

Then they had to speak to the fishermen who were allegedly buying the pictures. Just how big could this get? Sadie had a horrible feeling that they had only just scratched the surface.

And yet, they were no closer to finding out anything about the woman in the hold. That, Sadie reminded herself, was her priority. Murder was her specialty and not, thank God, child pornography.

Unless, of course, it indeed transpired that they overlapped.

Caz passed her a glass full of Scotch, and Sadie took a huge gulp, closing her eyes as the liquid burned its way down her throat and warmed her belly. When she opened them, Caz was watching her.

"I won't even ask what you've been working on today, because I know you can't tell me," Caz said, "but whatever it is, you obviously need that drink. You look like shit."

Sadie half laughed and half choked on her drink.

"Thanks," she said. "Nothing like a bit of brutal honesty, hey?"

Caz shrugged. "That's what I'm known for. Seriously though, you look terrible. Have you eaten? I've got some muffins in the back."

"Not since breakfast, but I'm okay," Sadie told the other woman, smiling at her kindness. The last thing she felt like was food. She was lying about breakfast too; that morning, neither she nor the Coopers had been able to eat a thing. The memory of the crab eaten body was still too fresh in their minds.

"You need fattening up," Caz said, looking over Sadie's petite frame. "You'll never find Prince Charming this way."

Sadie laughed again, although this time her laughter had a brittle edge to it. "I'm not looking for any princes, charming or otherwise," she said. "In my experience, the charming ones usually turn out to be psychopathic serial killers. It kind of puts you off after a while."

"I bet," Caz said, peering at her sympathetically. "I can't imagine how tough your job must be. Still," she said, her face brightening, "at least you get to work with Logan. Now he is a bit of eye candy that I wouldn't kick out of the bedroom." She winked at Sadie, who didn't know whether to laugh or squirm as the image of Cooper's naked and wounded but admittedly eye-catching torso flashed into her mind.

"The Sheriff?" she said. "He's just a colleague."

"Oh, come on," Caz said, rolling her eyes. "Surely you're not so jaded you can't recognize a handsome man when you see one. You know what you need?"

"Go on," Sadie said warily.

"To get laid, and laid *good*." Caz burst out laughing. Sadie shook her head, grinning weakly.

"It's been a long time," she admitted. "But again, the things you see and hear in this job can put you off that as well."

Or maybe it's just me, Sadie thought. Relationships were not her forte.

"It sounds lonely," Caz said, with a genuine empathy in her eyes that made Sadie feel touched by the other woman's concern, but also caused her a sudden pang of grief.

She had felt lonely ever since Jessica had gone. It was a visceral ache that never truly left her, whether she was with someone or not, hooked up or single. She still felt the loss of her sister every day.

"It can be," Sadie said, then swiftly changed the subject. "But it can't be much more fun running this place."

"Oh, I love it," Caz said. "But you're right, Prince Charming isn't going to be coming by these parts any time soon. And unfortunately, I don't think I'm the Sheriff's type. You, on the other hand," she winked again, and Sadie felt herself blush.

"Stop," she protested. "That's never going to happen."

Caz sat down on a stool opposite her and poured Sadie another drink, a single this time, then poured herself one too.

"That's on the house," Caz said. "We can drown our sorrows at being single, lonely Alaskan women together."

"You really know how to cheer a girl up, don't you Caz?" Sadie said ruefully.

They drank.

*

Sadie let herself in to the motel, tiptoeing through the reception. She was relieved to see the owner wasn't up to chide her for coming in way past the time stated on the guest rules board. The motel owner was a sour-faced old lady who treated her guests as though they were a hindrance rather than paying customers. The inside of the motel smelled stale, and moth eaten. Sadie had gone for the cheapest place rather than the most luxurious, while she looked for a more permanent place to stay.

Still, it was warm, and that was something after the bitter cold outside. She was craving a hot shower and clean – well, cleanish – sheets.

As she walked past the desk, her own name caught Sadie's eye and she looked down to see a large envelope next to a note from the clerk showing that the letter had been signed for that afternoon. Sadie picked it up, her stomach suddenly fizzing with anxiety. She had an awful feeling that she knew exactly what this was.

Holding the letter as though it was a bomb that might go off in her hand at any minute, Sadie made her way to her room.

She sat on the edge of the bed, staring down at the envelope and willing herself to open it.

She had, she realized, been waiting for this. She just hadn't expected it to come so soon. She opened the letter carefully, her stomach twisting further when she saw the letterhead.

It was from the FBI headquarters in Quantico.

Holding her breath, she scanned the letter. Then, not wanting to believe what she was reading, she read it again, more slowly, and the words and their implications sank in.

It seemed that her night could get worse after all.

Quantico needed an in-person statement regarding the shooting from her last case in D.C., where Sadie had shot and killed the suspect. At the time, Sadie had filled out all the obligatory reports that always followed such an event and given her statement. The suspect had been shot in self-defense, and Sadie had followed FBI protocol.

That's what she had told them, anyway. She had hoped that would be an end to it, and that she would be able to put that last case, which had so nearly destroyed her, behind her for good.

If her unanswered questions over Jessica's death had been the pull factor in her return to Alaska, it had been that last case and its culmination that had been the push. She hadn't been able to face staying in Washington, D.C., after that.

For the second time in her life, Sadie had run away.

Since her return to Alaska, she had put it out of her mind. There had been so much else to think about. Now it seemed that Quantico wanted to bring it all back up again.

Because she was being investigated.

According to the letter, more facts about the shooting had surfaced.

Facts that didn't match Sadie's original statement.

Which meant that they would need an in-person statement from her, to go over her account in light of the new 'facts.' The letter didn't specify when and where, only that they would be in touch. It was terse and to the point, giving away nothing, least of all as to the substance of the new 'facts.' Which left her knowing nothing about the questions they would be asking, or even how long she had to prepare.

As Sadie set the letter down on the bed next to her, her hands were shaking. Although on some level she had been expecting this, the more time that had elapsed since the shooting, the more she had convinced herself that it was a closed case. That she would be able to move on and put it behind her.

But now that wasn't going to be an option.

Sadie stood up and shrugged off her jacket, trying to think coherently through her now scattered thoughts. As she took off her holster, she stared at her gun, then took it out and stared at it some more, feeling as though she was almost in a trance. She weighed it in her hands, feeling its familiar shape, and remembering how her hand had closed around it as she had pointed it at the man in Washington.

She remembered how she had stared down the barrel of the gun, looking at him and in one swift moment, making her decision.

He deserved to die.

Her memories were as vivid now as though she was back there, her fingers closing around the trigger. It took just a few seconds to fire a gun and take a man's life. A whole life extinguished in just a few moments of time.

She heard the gunshot, and saw the man drop to the ground, watching as his blood pumped out of the wound. His life's blood, leaving him. At the time, she had felt nothing. She had done what needed to be done. Now, as Sadie placed her gun down on the bed, she had tears in her eyes.

No matter where she ran to, Washington or Alaska, it seemed that the past had a habit of catching up with her.

And she was going to have to face it.

CHAPTER TWELVE

Although it had only been a week since she had walked into the Anchorage FBI Field Office, it felt like a lot longer. Having only spoken to the ASAC, Paul Golightly, once in the flesh, Sadie felt uncharacteristically nervous as she waited for him to join her in the office. A fresh-faced young agent had shown her through, peering at Sadie curiously. It occurred to Sadie that so far, she knew the Coopers and local State Troopers better than she did her own field agents.

"Price, good to see you," Golightly said as he came in. His sandy hair was thinning on the top, but other than that he looked younger than his over sixty decades. He was an Alaskan, born and bred, and he looked as though he would be more at home in the wilderness than behind a desk.

"You too, Sir," Sadie said politely. She wondered if he had gotten wind of her upcoming investigation, and she felt on edge, waiting for him to mention it. To question her and demand an explanation as to why his hotshot new agent was now under scrutiny by the head honchos at Quantico.

Instead, he nodded at her, a smile in his eyes.

"You did good out there, Price. Did us proud. I sent you straight out on a case and you nailed it. I hear even Sheriff Cooper is impressed."

"Thank you, Sir," she said quietly. The impression that she garnered so far from Golightly was that of a man who didn't give praise easily. With an inward sigh of relief, she guessed that he hadn't yet been informed about the investigation.

"So," he went on, "now that I've blown some smoke up your ass, what's going on up at the harbor?"

"I wish I knew," Sadie said with a heavy sigh. Golightly frowned.

"You having trouble up there? The Coopers giving you a hard time?"

"No," Sadie said, shaking her head. "In fact, the Sheriff and myself seem to have buried any differences. For now, anyway. I'm just struggling to get a handle on this case; it seems to be going off in all directions."

"So, tell me about it."

Golightly leaned back in his chair and crossed his hands behind his head, waiting. Sadie gave him a brief report on the still unidentified body in the hold, the discovery of the pictures and the arrest of Joe Higgins, and the additional information that she had gotten from Johnny. Golightly listened intently, tapping his foot against his desk.

"What are your thoughts?" he asked when she had finished. "The woman knew something about the kiddie porn, so Higgins silenced her?"

"Maybe," Sadie said with a frown, wondering if it could be that simple. The woman's tongue had been cut out…was that a warning, to anyone else who might be thinking about becoming a snitch? It seemed too much for the small-scale operation that Higgins was running, but as she and Cooper had speculated, that could well be just the tip of an iceberg.

"Tell me what you're thinking, Price," Golightly said. "What do your instincts say?"

"Honestly? Not a lot, right now. My first thought, when the ME mentioned the tongue, was that we were looking at a potential serial. That the killer took the tongue as a trophy. But your theory is the most obvious one; it could be a warning not to talk, which I would say points to more than a few pictures of local girls, not that they aren't disgusting enough by themselves."

Golightly nodded, although he was still looking at her with that keen, sharp look of his, which made her feel slightly uncomfortable. She could easily imagine him in the interrogation room, staring down a suspect until they cracked.

"You don't think Higgins is our guy, do you?" he asked her eventually. Sadie ran a hand through her hair, thinking.

"No," she said eventually, "I don't. The way that she was killed, the tongue…Higgins is a nasty piece of work, but I'm not convinced this is him. It doesn't mean that he isn't connected though. I need to focus on the body rather than the pictures, at least until we know for sure whether they are linked. But until we know who she is…," Sadie shrugged. Golightly would know as well as she did just how many dead people turned up that were never identified or claimed. Undocumented immigrants, the homeless, addicts and prostitutes; people that the world had forgotten.

She thought about the poor woman in the hold, who as yet had no name or face, no identity, and vowed that if it was within her power, then she would get justice for what had been done to her.

"I'll put another agent on with you," Golightly offered. "Most of my best agents are on this meth ring up at Eagle River, but you could take O'Hara. He needs the experience."

Sadie remembered the eager young agent from her first day in Anchorage. He seemed pleasant enough, but Sadie preferred to work alone, and she only just got used to the Coopers. Another Fed would rattle the Sheriff, and Sadie didn't have the time to supervise a younger agent on a complex case.

"I don't want to risk my truce with the Sheriff," she said carefully, "and I don't think it's necessary yet. If the child abuse material turns out to be a much bigger ring, or bodies turn up outside the Sheriff's jurisdiction, that will be a different matter. However," she went on, "O'Hara could search the database for me. Any similar cases, in any state, of bodies turning up at harbors, especially with body parts missing. Just in case my hunch about a serial is right."

"Are your hunches usually right?" Golightly asked her.

"Unfortunately," Sadie said with a shudder, "yes." She stood up to leave.

"Well, you will soon find out Price," he told her as she was on her way out of the door, "depending on whether another body turns up or not."

*

Sadie walked into the Station House to find Cooper already waiting for her, no doubt eager to question Higgins. The Sheriff looked drawn, as though he had barely slept, and she wondered if his stitches were acting up or whether the case was getting to him. Or, most likely, a combination of both. It had been a rough few days for both of them.

"The duty lawyer is here. She's in with Higgins now," he told her.

"Before we question him," Sadie began, "I went back to the harbor last night and…"

"I know," Cooper cut in. "It was good work. Johnny Guthrie came in with his mom and his social worker first thing this morning and gave a statement against Higgins, as well as the names of the two fishermen that he was selling the pictures to."

In spite of his praise, he looked less than pleased with her actions, even if they had borne fruit.

"That's great," she said, "It was just a thought that was nagging me – how did we miss the pictures and the cash? I thought that if there was a hiding place, then we might also find something to link Higgins to the body."

"Good thinking, but don't you think you could have shared it? You don't work for me, Agent," Cooper said stiffly, "but it would be a nice idea to let me know before you go off on your own."

Sadie swallowed her first reaction, which was to bite back with a retort. "I'm sorry," she said again. "I'm used to working alone where possible. And I didn't want to disturb your rest for nothing. You were tired and had been badly hurt."

Cooper looked at her with a softness in his eyes that she wasn't expecting. "You could have been hurt too," he said. "A lot worse than a few lousy stitches," he said, gesturing towards his wounded torso and wincing with the movement. Those few lousy stitches were more painful than he was letting on.

"I hear you," Sadie said, blinking to hide her surprise. She had thought he was just angry at her for taking over on his case, but it seemed he was genuinely concerned for her welfare as well.

It was a nice feeling.

"Let's go and question Higgins," she said abruptly, not wanting to examine that feeling in too much detail. She walked off quickly towards the interview room with the Sheriff close behind her.

Higgins was sitting with a tall woman who had a sharp, black bob and was blessed with cheekbones that could cut glass. She stood up and stretched out her hand as Sadie came into the room, although her eyes went to the Sheriff, lingering briefly on him before returning to Sadie with a look of mild disdain.

"Erin Curtis," the woman said, in a cultured, Ivy League kind of voice that immediately made Sadie feel inferior. "I'll be acting as Mr. Higgins's lawyer. And you are?"

Sadie shook the woman's hand briskly, dropping it as quickly as was polite. "Federal Special Agent Price," she said and took her seat. Ms. Curtis sat down slowly, one perfectly plucked eyebrow raised.

"A Federal Agent? Is that really necessary?"

"We are talking about murder here, Ms. Curtis," Sadie said impatiently, guessing that the woman was going to be a hindrance. Of course, that was her job. She wondered what a lawyer as well educated as Ms. Curtis seemed to be was doing representing every lowlife that got hauled in up here. "And a particularly vicious one too. So yes, I would say my presence here is absolutely necessary."

The lawyer's eyes flickered to the Sheriff, as though she expected him to agree. Instead, Cooper said evenly, "Agent Price's expertise in these matters is considerable, Ms. Curtis. Your client has unfortunately been less than forthcoming."

"That's because," the lawyer said, tapping her nails on the table, "my client is innocent, as you know damn well. You don't have one real speck of evidence against him. Unless you have managed to turn up something overnight that suggests that he has killed anyone, then you need to release him."

Cooper glanced at Sadie. "Do you want to tell them or shall I?" he said. She suppressed a smile. "Go ahead, Sheriff," she said. Cooper turned towards Higgins and his lawyer.

"We don't have any evidence -yet – that you killed that woman, Higgins." He paused, waiting until Higgins looked relieved and Erin Curtis appeared faintly triumphant, before continuing, "However, we are charging you with both possession and distribution of child pornography. So, I'm afraid you aren't going anywhere just yet. You might want to start talking to Ms. Curtis here about your bail hearing."

Higgins eyes bulged in his face. "They're not mine!" he shouted. "You can't do this!"

"That's not what Johnny Guthrie says," Sadie cut in, watching the shock on Higgins's face with satisfaction. He opened his mouth like a fish and then looked at his lawyer in desperation.

"If I could have a moment with my client," Ms. Curtis said. Sadie looked at Cooper, who nodded. She followed him out of the room. They turned to each other, and Sadie was about to speak, when the Trooper that had been on the front desk called for the Sheriff.

"There's been a call from the 911 Dispatch you're going to want to know about," the Trooper said. He was an older guy, with a deerskin hat and a bushy beard. Sadie guessed that he was a part-timer, one of the locals with a good sense of his civic duty.

"Go on," Cooper said.

"There's been a body found down at the harbor," the Trooper said. Sadie felt her skin go cold as Golightly's parting words came back to her.

"In one of the crab holds?" Cooper asked. The Trooper nodded.

Sadie felt sick.

“Was it a woman?” she asked, briefly closing her eyes against the images of the first body. Not that it would make any difference, when the images were in her head.

“Yes, a woman,” the Trooper confirmed.

Sadie took a breath and looked at Cooper. “We had better get down to the harbor,” she said.

Higgins and the fancy lawyer could wait.

CHAPTER THIRTEEN

Sadie followed the Sheriff onto the *Mustang Sally*, bracing herself for what she was about to see. The forensics team was already there, and the hold had been cordoned off. Three fishermen and the captain stood by the bridge, waiting for them. The captain looked impatient, as though he had better things to be doing and couldn't afford to be held up by bodies turning up on his boat. Sadie supposed there was plenty of truth in that; it was prime fishing season and time was money.

The captain introduced himself and pointed to one of his men. "This is Mike DaCosta," he said. "He's the one you want to speak to; it was him who found the woman."

Sadie felt Cooper's eyes briefly turn towards her. Mike DaCosta was one of the names that Johnny Guthrie had given them as being a buyer of the pictures. She felt her heart rate quicken even as she questioned the fact that this was too neat a situation to be true. Surely, if he was the killer, he wouldn't risk being the one to find her?

Unless he hadn't had much choice. There couldn't be much time to get the women into the hold in between the harbor coming alive and boats going out to sea. Perhaps it had been unavoidable.

"We will speak to Mr. DaCosta," Cooper told the captain. "But first, it would be helpful if we could see a ship's manifest?"

The captain folded his arms. He hadn't even looked at Sadie. "Why?" he asked.

"If you could talk us through what happened, Mr. DaCosta?" the Sheriff said.

DaCosta licked his lips and as he began to speak, his nerves were palpable. His eyes darted from side to side, pausing to linger over the view of the harbor. Without having consciously thought about it, Sadie realized that she had shifted position, ready for something to happen.

"Mr. DaCosta?" Cooper prompted.

"There isn't much to say," the man said finally. Sadie caught a trace of a Southern accent in his voice. This guy wasn't Alaskan; in fact, he was very far from home. "I was the first one down into the hold to clear the catch out. I saw a hand, so I moved a few of the crabs out of the way. I didn't expect it to be a body, I thought it would be a doll or a mannequin or something. Sometimes the catches dredge up some weird stuff. As soon as I saw what it was, I was out of there. I told the others to keep away, and the captain called 911."

"Thank you," Cooper said. "Is there anything else you can think of that might be important?"

"Yeah. I don't know how she got in there." He said it defensively and his eyes swung to Sadie, only to go wide as he took in her badge.

"You're FBI?" he said, and took a small step backwards, his gaze darting around again as though looking for an escape. He was ready to run, Sadie realized.

Cooper spotted it too and stepped forward, towards the man, blocking his path to the bridge. "Mr. DaCosta, we would appreciate it if you could come down to the station with us," he said. "There are a few things that we need to ask you."

"About the body?"

"And a few other things," Cooper said.

DaCosta moved so fast that he was almost off the boat and onto the dock before Sadie or the Sheriff had time to react. Sadie cursed as she began to run after him. The Sheriff followed, close behind her at first and then overtaking her just in time to make a grab for DaCosta, right as the man tried to vault over the side of the boat.

DaCosta kicked out hard and his boot made contact with Cooper's face. Cooper stumbled backwards, knocking into Sadie and pushing her into the side of the boat so hard that it knocked the wind out of her momentarily and she doubled over.

It afforded DaCosta precious time, and before Sadie could make it off the boat and onto the harbor, he was running down towards the private fishing boats at the end of the dock. Realizing what he was about to do, she yelled after him to stop and put his hands up, even though she knew there was little chance of him complying.

DaCosta was a man who clearly didn't want to be caught.

Sadie sped up, pumping her thighs as fast as she could and wishing that she hadn't let her fitness regime lapse in recent weeks. Again, Cooper overtook her.

"He's going to try and escape on one of the smaller boats," Sadie yelled ahead to the Sheriff.

There was a crowd of people watching them now, from the various dockhands to fishermen who had come ashore or crowded to the sides of their own boats to see what was happening. A few of them cheered

DaCosta on, taking the side of someone they saw as one of their own against the cops. None of them were about to help, that was for sure – but then, they didn't realize what was at stake.

Sadie and the Sheriff were just yards away from DaCosta when he boarded a small boat, and Sadie stopped and watched in horror as he fired the engine. Cooper yelled in frustration as he skidded to a stop just in front of her.

Sadie eyed up the boat next to the one that DaCosta had taken. Its shocked-looking captain stared back at them.

"Come on," Sadie said to Cooper, jumping aboard the captain's boat. "Let's get after him."

She wasn't going to let DaCosta escape. Not on her watch.

The captain shook his head as she approached, already guessing what she was going to say, but Sadie had no time to argue. She flashed her badge quickly.

"Special Agent Sadie Price," she said, "and we're commandeering this launch. We have a fugitive on the run."

The captain put his hands up, looking panicked and unsure of what to do.

"You're not in any trouble," Cooper assured him from behind Sadie. "But we need this boat."

"But I've just had the paintwork done," he protested. Sadie ignored him and ran to the wheel, staring at it. She had never captained a boat in her life.

"I've got it," the Sheriff said, taking over. The captain had jumped ashore, not wanting to get involved in chasing after DaCosta, but he was wringing his hands in despair over his boat as he watched them. Sadie felt a moment's sympathy for him. The poor guy had probably just wanted to do a day's fishing.

Cooper started the engine and they sped away from the dock after DaCosta, fast enough that Sadie felt her stomach launch and she grabbed hold of the side. She had never been a fan of being on the water; she preferred solid ground to be beneath her feet.

The Sheriff, however, handled the boat like a natural and Sadie looked at him in admiration. "You know what you're doing," she said, a statement rather than a question. Cooper heard the approval in her voice and smiled, even though his eyes were fixed on DaCosta in the distance.

"I used to go fishing with my dad as a kid, on his rare days off. He used to say it was the only thing that took his mind off work." Sadie knew that Cooper's dad had been a cop, too. The Coopers seemed to have had an idyllic upbringing compared to Sadie's, although there were times when Sadie was sure that the Sheriff had secrets of his own too.

Everyone had their skeletons, after all.

"You're fast, too," she said, remembering how he had twice caught up with her as they had chased DaCosta on foot.

"I used to run track in high school back in Juneau. I was a bit of a jock," he said, not entirely without pride.

"That figures," Sadie said. "I can see you as a jock. It fits you perfectly."

Cooper frowned. "I have no idea whether that is meant as a compliment or not, so I'll take it as one," he said. "Now, where the hell is this guy heading? Surely he's not crazy enough to take us out on the open sea?"

Sadie watched as DaCosta headed directly away from the harbor, which was already a speck in the distance.

"I hope not," she said, wincing as the spray from a large wave that slapped the side of the boat hit her face. "The sea is as choppy as hell." She braced herself on the deck as it rolled again, not relishing the thought of ending up in the icy water.

"We may have to radio through for a helicopter," the Sheriff said. "If he is making for the open seas, I doubt that we can catch him."

"I think he's changing his position," Sadie said. "The direction he's taking; look, he's following the coastline."

Cooper nodded as he leaned on the wheel. "He knows where he's going," he guessed. "He's going to try and disembark somewhere."

"There are some small islands up ahead," Sadie said. "Although they barely warrant the name 'island.' More like outcrops of rock. But if he gets off on one of them then he's going to leave himself cornered. He would be better off making a break for it, although I suspect he knows that he's going to get caught either way. He's panicking."

If he was panicking, then he would make rash decisions. Which could make him dangerous.

"Do you think he's armed?" Cooper said, echoing her thoughts.

"Probably not, if he was working on the boats all night, but we are," Sadie replied. "He's got no chance. We're going to bring him in." A thought flitted across the edges of her mind, nagging at her that something was wrong. That they had missed something that could be important, but she couldn't quite grasp the thought.

"You were right about the islands. He's heading towards that outcropping." Cooper jerked his head towards an outgrowth of rock that now loomed ahead through the fog. As they got closer, Sadie could see a small, rundown shack, and she felt herself go cold.

"He knows where he's going," she said. "He's been here before. That shack could be where he's taking the victims."

The Sheriff nodded grimly. "The idiot is leading us right to the evidence."

"He's got a weapon there," Sadie guessed. "He's luring us in."

Up ahead, DaCosta beached his boat on the island and jumped ashore. Just as they thought, he made straight for the shack, not even bothering to look behind him to see how close they were.

"Hold on," Cooper said as he made straight for the outcropping. The deck rolled and lurched sharply as Cooper beached their boat in turn, and Sadie heard rocks banging against the side and guessed that the poor captain's paintwork was likely to be ruined.

She vaulted over the side, landing harshly on the sandy rocks, and drew her gun as she made her way towards the shack in a defensive crouch. In moments, Cooper was right beside her with his own weapon drawn.

"DaCosta," he yelled. "This is Sheriff Cooper. We need you to put down any weapons and turn yourself in. I repeat, we need you to come in."

In answer, a rifle shot cracked through the air. They both threw themselves down on the ground. Sadie rolled away towards the shelter of a large rock and then looked around for Cooper as another shot rang out. Her stomach lurched as she saw the second bullet only narrowly miss him.

In seconds he was at her side, shielded by the rock. Once again, he called to DaCosta. "Put your weapons down! Come out with your hands in the air!"

He ducked as another shot rang out. Sadie set her jaw stubbornly.

"Bastard," she hissed. "I'm going in. Cover me."

"No," the Sheriff snapped. "We don't know what's going on in there. I'm going to radio for back-up."

"He's one guy," Sadie protested. She could feel the adrenaline running through her, the thrill of the chase. She wanted to bring DaCosta in and put an end to all this.

Then a thought occurred to her.

"There could be other victims in there," she said. "Possibly alive."

Cooper looked at her, his eyes wide. Then he radioed for back-up.

"We have a fugitive situation," he barked before giving their location. "It looks like we have just found our killer."

CHAPTER FOURTEEN

The minutes ticked by agonizingly slowly as Sadie kept her eyes on the window of the shack where DaCosta had been shooting from. Since the back-up had arrived – the coastguards and a few deputized townspeople – DaCosta had gone quiet.

With the back-up crew forming a ring around the perimeter of the shack, there was no way that DaCosta could escape, and Sadie wondered just how long he could realistically keep this up for. It had only been just over an hour, but out here in the bitter cold, it felt like all day. She didn't relish the prospect of being stuck out here at night. Maybe that was his plan, to stay put until they all froze to death.

The Sheriff had a bullhorn now, but his efforts to negotiate with DaCosta had only been met with silence. He was also refusing to let them know if there was anyone else inside. Next to Sadie, Cooper was getting impatient too.

"We should have rushed him after all," he grumbled, clapping his hands together for warmth. One of the townspeople had brought a flask of hot coffee, which Sadie didn't think she had ever been so grateful for. Cooper looked drawn, with dark shadows under his eyes, and she guessed that the chase had hurt his freshly stitched wound, not that he would admit it to her.

"No, you were right. I was being hasty," Sadie admitted. "We are both itching to bring him in, but this is a delicate situation."

The thought that had been nagging away at her finally emerged into her consciousness. "Cooper," she said slowly, "are we even sure that this guy is the killer?"

The Sheriff looked startled. "Seriously Price? He ran before we could even finish questioning him about the body. Now he's holed up in a shack shooting at us. He clearly had ammo stored there. What else could he be using it for?"

"I don't know," Sadie admitted. "But didn't his captain say that the boat had been out all night? Which means he hid the girl before his shift and then spent all night on the boat, knowing that she could be discovered, and that he could be the one to find her? I know I said killers like to be close to the scene of the crime, but this is just not sitting right with me."

"He has to be involved somehow," the Sheriff countered. "He wouldn't be hiding in there and aiming at police officers unless he was running from something big." They both looked at the shack, perched precariously on top of a clump of rock as though a giant hand had put it down and forgotten about it. It would, Sadie thought with a shudder, be the perfect place for the killer to take and hide his victims.

It had to be DaCosta.

"But then how is he bringing them here?" she wondered aloud. "If he doesn't have a boat of his own?"

"It's about the child abuse material then; it must be," Cooper said. "Perhaps he's the ringleader. Johnny isn't the sharpest tool in the box; I doubt he knows what is truly going on there."

"Right now, none of us do," Sadie said. "If we could just get DaCosta's ass out here, it might help us get some answers. If he's still in there by nightfall, we should go in."

"Why not before? We won't be able to see what the hell we're doing in the dark. There's not much light here in the winter as it is. We should take advantage of what little we've got."

They both went back to staring at the shack, having reached a stalemate, when Deputy Cooper came through on the Sheriff's radio. Back at the station, she had been tasked with searching the database for any information on Mike DaCosta.

"I've found him," she said triumphantly, her voice on the line crackling. "No wonder he ran as soon as he saw you. Sadie's boss will be happy; the Feds have been looking for him for months, ever since he dropped off their radar."

Sadie leaned towards the radio so that she could hear the Deputy better. "Go on," she said, her stomach tightening.

"He has got warrants out in four states," Deputy Jane Cooper told them. "A total nasty piece of work. His real name is Manuel DaSilva, but he also frequently goes by Mike DaCosta, Jorge Solano, and Karl Del'Olio. You would think that he would have come up with a new persona this time, but I guess he thought that Alaska was far enough away to be safe."

Sadie nodded to herself. The fishing trade was a good bet to attempt to hide in; workers were often undocumented and paid in cash. Untraceable.

"What is he wanted for?" the Sheriff asked.

"It would be quicker for me to tell you what he isn't wanted for," the Deputy replied. "He's got warrants going back years for weapons smuggling, dealing in crystal meth, kidnapping and sexual assault of his ex-girlfriend and, most recently, sex trafficking a minor. It seems he has upped his game."

"He fits the right profile," Sadie murmured. Something still told her that it wasn't quite right, but she pushed the thought away. It didn't matter in this very moment; the fact was that DaCosta was a lowlife who needed to be brought in.

"If this goes on much longer, I will need to call Golightly and get other agents in," Sadie told the Sheriff. "His warrants cross four states; it's a federal affair."

Cooper glared at the shack stubbornly. "I haven't been shot at and sitting here freezing my ass off for nothing," he retorted. "Give me a chance to negotiate with him. We still need to know his involvement with the pictures, as well as the murders."

Sadie nodded. "Go ahead. He's more likely to talk to you than he is to me. Just don't get shot; we've had enough trips to the hospital lately."

Cooper grinned ruefully and stood up from behind the rock, his bullhorn in one hand and his gun in the other.

"Mr. DaCosta," he yelled. "We are aware of your outstanding warrants. The longer you hide from us, the worse it is going to be for you. If you cooperate, you might just be able to cut a deal. You are not going to get away from here DaCosta; we've got you surrounded. Why don't you let us in, and we can talk?"

Sadie saw the outline of a man's head at the small window in the shack. "I'm not talking to that Fed bitch," he yelled.

"Just me, then," the Sheriff offered. "Let me in and we'll talk. All I need is to ask you a few questions about the body in the crab hold."

"That's got nothing to do with me," DaCosta yelled. "I don't know anything about it."

"Then let me in and let's see what kind of deal we can cut," Cooper said. "It's your only option, DaCosta. I'm your friend right now."

There was silence.

"Let him think about it," Sadie suggested as Cooper raised the bullhorn to his lips again. "He won't want to lose face by capitulating too early."

Cooper waited, and they both stared at the shack, willing DaCosta to give them an answer.

Until he did.

Another gunshot rang out, but although Sadie instinctively ducked, as she straightened up, she realized that the shot had come from inside the shack.

"Oh God," she gasped, feeling sick. "If he did have a victim in there then he has just shot her." She drew her gun and started to walk in a crouch towards the shack. After warning an unresponsive DaCosta that they were coming in, Cooper followed her.

"Either that," the Sheriff murmured as they approached the door, "or he's shot himself."

Only silence answered them.

With her back pressed up against the shack, next to the door, Sadie spun around and kicked the door open, her gun in front of her.

Ready to shoot.

"Hands up!" she yelled.

But there was no one to answer her.

On the floor in front of her lay Mike DaCosta. He was on his front with his leg splayed out at a funny angle, his rifle half stuck under his body.

Sadie didn't expect any answer from him.

The back of his head had been blown off.

CHAPTER FIFTEEN

"Nothing," Sadie said to herself in frustration as she finished going through the forensics from the shack. No fingerprints had been found that didn't belong to Mike DaCosta – or whatever his name was – and no trace of anything that could have belonged to either of the victims or that would even indicate their presence there.

There was zero evidence, just as Sadie had suspected, that DaCosta was their killer. As for Johnny's statement that he had been purchasing child pornography from Higgins, that statement was currently all that they had. DaCosta was no longer around for them to question.

It was possible that DaCosta had little to nothing to do with either case and had only run due to his outstanding warrants. In which case, they had spent their morning chasing the wrong guy, only for him to wind up dead. Which meant another report. Although Sadie knew that she held no culpability for DaCosta's suicide, it still cast a shadow over her while she was under investigation for the shooting of a suspect.

She stood up, tied her hair back more tightly into its braid and prepared herself to go down to the ME's office, not wanting to think about the state that the second body could be in. She just hoped that they could put an identity to this victim; because so far, they were getting nowhere.

Cooper was waiting for her, and Sadie suspected that he didn't want to go down on his own, remembering his reaction to the first body.

"We're seeing a lot of dead bodies lately," he said. Sadie nodded in response. There didn't seem to be anything else that she could say.

As they approached, Pete waved a gloved hand in greeting. "We meet again," he said.

Neither Sadie nor the Sheriff responded, and there was a despondent atmosphere as Pete began his litany of the wounds on the body.

It was bad, but thankfully not as bad as the first one. This victim still had some semblance of a face, at least, although the crabs had made quick work of her eyeballs and the soft skin of her lips. She had a large mole near what was once her top lip, and Sadie wondered if it had bothered her, and if she had ever wanted to have it removed. It seemed an odd thought, but it was those little details that brought the victim back to life, restoring them back to more than a lifeless hunk of flesh upon a slab.

"Same cause of death?" Cooper asked. Sadie noticed that he was avoiding having to look at the eyeless and lipless face.

"Yes, I'm afraid so," Pete said shortly, "although judging by the levels of benzodiazepines in her blood, I would say that she was unconscious throughout."

"That's a mercy, at least," Sadie said. "So, do you think he gave her a larger dose?"

"Either that, or she was found earlier," Pete said. "I would tentatively suggest that she was given the sedatives no earlier than yesterday afternoon. So, you have a timeframe to work with, at least."

"That helps," Cooper said, but Sadie shrugged.

"Not necessarily," she cautioned. "He could have abducted her well before that. Are there any signs of a struggle, or any restraint?" she asked Pete, who shook his head to indicate 'no.'

"Her tongue is also missing," he said. "Again, it's a deliberate incision, removed cleanly, with a very sharp knife."

Sadie glanced at the victim's mouth. "So, it isn't just body parts he is collecting; it's definitely something specific about the tongue."

"Trying to stop them speaking," Cooper said, finally turning his gaze towards the dead woman's face. "This has to be about the child abuse, surely?"

"It's one hell of a coincidence if it isn't," Sadie acknowledged. "But until we know more, coincidences are really all we have." She shook her head in frustration, knowing that although Cooper's theory made a logical kind of sense, just as it had when Golightly had suggested it, it just didn't click into place for her. The tongues were trophies; she felt sure of it. It was too personal; this wasn't just about sending a warning or punishing the weak links in some kind of pedophile ring. Her years of experience hunting some of the sickest minds a cop could encounter had honed her instincts, and they were screaming at her now.

Whoever this guy was, he wasn't done.

And he wouldn't stop unless they stopped him.

"There has to be a link between the victims," she said, scanning the body. "As far as I can tell, they look similar. Same long brown hair, similar build?" She looked across the body at Pete, who nodded.

"Yes. And you'll both be pleased to know that we managed to get intact fingerprints from this one. I've sent them over so that you can check the database. This one looks as though she could be Filipina, or similar, so if she has been through Immigration then you might get a valid ID for her."

Sadie felt a tingle of anticipation in her belly that they may actually get a breakthrough on the second victim. They certainly needed one. As it stood, one suspect was dead, and there was nothing to indicate that he even was truly a suspect. It had turned out that DaCosta had been at sea for two days when the first victim was discovered, so it was incredibly unlikely it could be him. As for Higgins, he was in custody and so he couldn't have killed the girl currently on the slab. They desperately needed some new information.

"Let's go and find out, shall we?" she said to Cooper. "Unless there's anything else you can tell us, Pete?"

The Medical Examiner shook his head. "That's about it for now," he said. "But if anything else comes up, I'll let you know. Otherwise, she will be going down to the morgue."

Sadie virtually jogged back up the stairs, praying to anyone that was listening that the database would yield some results.

She watched as Cooper fired up the old computer, praying again that the internet connected. It wouldn't be the first time an investigation had been stalled due to the terrible local signals, especially in the midwinter weather.

"Have you ever thought of investing in some better equipment?" she asked as she sat down at the monitor and the screen flickered to life.

"Local budgets are tight," Cooper said shortly. "Perhaps you guys could lend us some of yours?"

"Touché," Sadie murmured. Her fingers flew over the keys as she entered her details to give her access to the interstate database, bringing up the file that had been sent over from forensics.

"Anything?" Cooper asked impatiently. He was leaning over her shoulder, just as eager for results as she was, and Sadie was acutely aware of his warm breath next to her cheek. She could smell his cologne, a woody, musky smell that suited him.

"Give me a chance," she said. They both stared at the screen, grinning simultaneously as it flashed up with a match.

"Bingo," Sadie said, clicking on the file. "Here we go."

From over her shoulder, Cooper read out the information on the screen, next to an image of a young and pretty woman with a large mole above her top lip.

"Carmen Mila. Twenty-three years old, from the Philippines. And... check this out. She came over to work as an au pair."

Sadie swiveled round in her chair to face him, her heart hammering in her chest. This could be it. They had found the link.

"The kids in the pictures," she said, and saw the same realization dawn on Cooper's face. "Do their parents employ au pairs?"

"I'll need to speak to Jane. With all the distraction with DaCosta and the body, we haven't had the chance to touch base," he said, reaching for his phone and walking to the other side of the room to call his sibling.

Sadie strained to hear what the Deputy was saying, but the Sheriff's face when he ended the call told her everything that she needed to know.

"One of the girls from the photographs is Lily Randolph," he said. "She had an au pair called Carmen. Mrs. Randolph said that Carmen hasn't been seen since yesterday morning. It was her afternoon off, but she didn't come back last night. Jane thinks the parents didn't know about the pictures. Until we found them. Mr. Randolph accused Carmen of having something to do with them; he said to Jane that he has never trusted the au pair. But the kid is refusing to speak."

Sadie jumped up, grabbing her coat from the back of the chair. It looked as though Cooper was right about the tongues after all.

"Then we need to go and speak to the Randolphs right now," she said.

*

Cooper pulled up outside a house large enough that it could only be described as a mansion, and Sadie's eyebrows shot up her forehead at the sight.

"Nice," she said. "What is it that the Randolphs do exactly?"

"He's a huge name in the trucking industry," Cooper told her. "His wife, as far as I know, doesn't work, but she's very active in Anchorage. On the school board, active at church, that type of thing. Jane said that they both seemed more concerned about the locals finding out about the pictures than Lily herself. They were horrified when Jane said that a social worker would be visiting."

"Do you think they had anything to do with it? Parents are the usual culprits – but caregivers would be a close second. Maybe Carmen and Mr. Randolph were in it together – which could make him a suspect in her murder." Sadie's mind was whirring with the possibilities that this new information presented, but Cooper gave her a sharp look.

"Might well be the case," he said, "but go easy until we have some evidence to back that up, okay? This guy could bring a team of lawyers down on our heads if we put a foot out of place. This isn't the time to go barging in with direct accusations."

"As if I would," Sadie said sweetly, ignoring Cooper's snort of disbelief. She followed him out of the snow cat and up the driveway towards the Randolphs' front door.

A woman with perfectly coiffed chestnut hair and far too much Botox opened the door. She clutched a hand to her chest theatrically as she saw the Sheriff.

"Oh, Logan," she said, on the verge of tears which seemed, to Sadie, to be somewhat put on for their benefit, "it's so good of you to come. We are in such a state about Lily. She's up in her room, refusing to eat, the poor thing."

"I'm so sorry to hear that, Mrs. Randolph," Cooper said politely, ignoring the use of his first name. "We need to ask you and your husband a few questions. Is Mr. Randolph here?"

"Yes," Mrs. Randolph said, looking worried. "Tony's working from our home office. But really, we've told your officers all that we know. Lily still won't say who took the pictures of her. I just can't believe it would be Carmen; she is just so sweet."

"It's Carmen we're here about, Ma'am," Sadie said politely. "If we could come in?"

Mrs. Randolph looked at Sadie for the first time, and then back at Cooper. "Another Trooper, Sheriff? I hoped that we could just deal with you and your sister. We don't want this all around town – for Lily's sake, of course."

"Actually, I'm a Special Agent with the BAU unit," Sadie said evenly, watching the woman's eyes go wide.

"FBI?" she hissed. "Is this really necessary?" Sadie was beginning to get pissed off with being asked that today.

Mrs. Randolph ushered them quickly inside to a large reception hall with marbled floors and a staircase leading to an open balcony. It was a lot grander than most of the homes in Anchorage, and certainly more so than the cabins out in the hinterlands where Sadie had been raised.

Sadie watched as the woman hurried off to fetch her husband, her totally impractical heels making a clacking noise on the marble tiles.

As they waited, Sadie looked around, noticing the pictures and mounts on the wall. Nautical prints, watercolors of ships and trophy catches adorned the walls.

It seemed that Mr. Randolph liked his fishing boats.

When he appeared, he looked nothing like Sadie had been expecting. Given the showy house and the trophy wife, she had been anticipating a larger than life, brash character, but Mr. Randolph was a small, weaselly looking man with a receding hairline, wearing undoubtedly expensive slacks that looked three sizes too big.

His eyes, however, showed a keen intelligence, and as he appraised Sadie coolly, she made a mental note to herself to not underestimate the man. He was no fool, and the way that his wife twitched around him, looking at him nervously, Sadie suspected that he was very much in charge at home as well as in his business.

"Lily's in her room, resting," he said, without bothering with greetings. "She's exhausted from being questioned earlier, and still hasn't told us anything. No doubt out of loyalty to that au pair. It can only be her; no one else has access to our daughter unsupervised." Rage flashed in his eyes, and Sadie couldn't help but sympathize, unable to imagine how it must feel to think that someone you had trusted with your child could have violated that trust so terribly.

Assuming that he was innocent himself, of course. Sadie was generally of the opinion that until there was evidence to show otherwise, then everyone was a suspect.

"It's Carmen we've come about," Cooper said again. "You said previously that the last time that you saw her was yesterday morning?"

"Yes," the man snapped, "But we've already been over this. She probably knew that she was about to get caught and ran off. I haven't got much faith in you lot to find her; I'll be employing a private detective."

"There won't be any need, Mr. Randolph," Sadie said, flashing her badge at the same time. "I'm afraid that Carmen was found dead this morning. We have reason to believe that she was murdered."

Mr. Randolph blinked rapidly, although his expression didn't change. His wife's hand flew to her mouth, and she whimpered. She looked genuinely distraught, Sadie thought. In spite of her polished appearance, the woman was a bag of nerves.

"Murdered? But who...?" She turned to her husband as though he might have the answers. "Tony?" she said. Mr. Randolph ignored her, instead pacing across the hall and back again. Sadie watched them both.

"We need to know both of your whereabouts yesterday," she said.

Tony Randolph glared at her. "We were both here all day, and the housekeeper and Lily can vouch for that," he said. "I suggest you tread carefully before you accuse me and my wife."

Sadie ignored Cooper's warning look. "We will need a statement from your housekeeper to confirm that," she said. "I'm not accusing anyone. It's simply routine."

"That's fine," the man snapped, clearly agitated and drumming his fingers on his thigh. "Then you can get on with finding out who did it. Not that I blame them, after what has happened to our daughter. It's hardly a loss, is it," he snapped, glaring at Sadie.

"We don't actually know that Carmen was involved yet, Sir," the Sheriff reminded him. "Although perhaps Lily will be more inclined to speak now that Carmen is dead."

Mrs. Randolph let out a sob. "I just can't take all this in," she whispered. "She seemed like such a sweet girl, so helpful and kind."

"Do you know where she was going yesterday, for her afternoon off?" Cooper asked. Mrs. Randolph shook her head. "No, but her laptop is up in her room. I know she was on it before she left. Perhaps that might help?" She addressed her question to her husband.

"You can take them upstairs," he said. "I'll go and break the news to Lily." He walked off without addressing them further, and Sadie and the Sheriff followed Mrs. Randolph upstairs.

Carmen's room was at the back of the house, small but still more luxurious than anywhere that Sadie had ever stayed, with a carpet deep enough to leave footprints and fresh, pure cotton sheets.

The room was tidy, with no photographs or trinkets to show that Carmen had ever been here. There was however a small, red laptop left open on the bedside table.

"Is that Carmen's?" Sadie asked. Mrs. Randolph nodded and then shut the door behind her, speaking in hushed tones.

"I didn't want to say in front of Tony," she said, "Because he thought I gave Carmen too much time off as it was, but…I think she had a date yesterday."

Sheriff Cooper and Sadie exchanged a glance. "A date? With who?" Sadie asked as she walked over to the laptop and turned it on.

"I don't know, she didn't tell me," Mrs. Randolph said nervously, wringing her hands. Her whole demeanor had changed now, and there were tears glimmering in the corners of her eyes. "I don't know how to feel," she said to Sadie, her tone imploring, as though Sadie could somehow make it all better. "Carmen was so sweet; I really relied on her. But to think she made Lily pose for those pictures…" She shook her head, the horror naked in her eyes. Sadie's heart went out to her as she realized that she had misjudged her. The woman might be pretentious and overly concerned with the neighbors, but her distress for her child was genuine.

"We will get to the bottom of this," she assured her. For the first time since the original body had been found, Sadie was starting to feel that the answers were right within their grasp. They didn't have all the pieces yet, but the few that they did have were starting to fit together.

She watched as the laptop came on, revealing a desktop with no password, and saw an open messenger app in the bottom right corner of the screen. "Here we go," she murmured, clicking on it. A stream of messages came up, and Sadie read quickly through them.

"It looks like Carmen arranged to meet some guy off the internet, on this app," she said. "There are messages going back a few weeks or more."

"Is there a name?" Cooper scanned the messages himself, frowning. "Just an anonymous username, and no profile. Why would she be stupid enough to go and meet him when he could be anyone?" he muttered to himself, sounding angry.

"There's no sign of the pictures, but I don't think that there will be on this device," Sadie said. "Not the way that she has just left it open with no password protection. Although there could be hidden files. These messages seem genuine though; just an internet hook-up app. Carmen wasn't using her real details either, look: she calls herself 'sexyaupair.' Not particularly subtle."

"What time does it say they were meeting?" Cooper asked. Sadie scrolled back through the more recent messages.

"Early evening, yesterday. At a café that's only a mile or so from the harbor." She bit her lip, feeling the adrenaline rising in her. "We've got our guy…we just don't know who he is. I can take the laptop to our Field Office and get our IT department on it, but it could take a few days," she said, the impatience showing in her voice.

"No need," Cooper said. "Jane is really good with this stuff. Let's give it to her first. She can meet us down at the station."

Sadie picked up the laptop as carefully as though it was made of precious metal. The innocuous looking gadget held the next piece to the puzzle and could lead them straight to the killer.

CHAPTER SIXTEEN

As Sadie watched Deputy Jane Cooper's fingers whizz across the keyboard of the au pair's laptop, she couldn't help thinking how weary the Deputy looked. The other woman had spent all day, apart from the dramatic interlude with DaCosta, liaising with Social Services and questioning the four local children that had been photographed naked, in poses that no child should even be aware of. The strain showed in her face, and Sadie didn't envy her; personally, she was more comfortable with half-eaten bodies.

"I think I can find the location that these messages were sent from," Jane murmured, her eyes fixed on the screen. "Just give me a few more minutes."

Sadie sat down opposite her. She felt full of nervous energy, and the strong coffee she was currently gulping wasn't helping. A strong whiskey from the saloon sounded tempting, even though she had never been a heavy drinker. Not after watching the way that her father's alcoholism had destroyed their family.

"There's something else that you need to know," the Deputy said as she worked. "Because it seems more and more likely that this whole thing is linked, doesn't it? Two of the kids interviewed this morning were only four and five years old, siblings. They didn't understand what those pictures were about, of course; they thought it was a game. With their au pair."

Sheriff Cooper sat down at the desk with a thump, looking stunned. "Jesus Christ," he said. "Have you brought her in?"

"The au pair? I can't," the Deputy responded, her mouth a grim line. "Because she hasn't been seen for three days. Apparently, she just took off with no warning."

There was a stunned silence as Sadie and the Sheriff took in this new information.

"Our first victim," Sadie said, her voice sounding loud in the small room. "Perhaps she went off on an internet date, too."

The Deputy suddenly gave a triumphant grin and turned the laptop around so that they could see the screen.

"We might be able to find out," she said. "The messages to Carmen were sent from here. He was using an internet café on the edge of town. Not far from the harbor, in fact."

*

The internet café consisted of a small cabin with eight terminals and a Barista serving coffee and hot chocolate. The Barista was a young guy who looked to be fresh out of college, who watched Sadie and the Sheriff warily as they walked around the room. Only two of the terminals were in use, one by a trio of giggling teenage girls, and another by an elderly man, a local that greeted Cooper with warmth before going back to Wikipedia.

"Erm, can I help you guys?" the Barista asked. Cooper strode to the counter.

"I'm the Sheriff," he said, flashing his badge. The young guy looked startled, then frankly bemused as Sadie joined them and introduced herself.

"Has something happened?" he asked. "Because honestly, this place is pretty boring. I make coffee, and reboot the computers when they go down, which happens a lot. That's about as exciting as it gets, I'm afraid."

"Is it your place?" Sadie asked, surprised when he nodded. He seemed too young to own his own business.

"Yep. There's just me and a friend helping out, but she has been on vacation this week, spending New Year with her folks. It's been quiet in here over the holiday season."

"Can you remember who was in here yesterday morning?" Cooper asked impatiently. The Barista shrugged.

"I can get you the list of terminals in use; we charge by the hour, so customers have to fill in time slots" he said. "But folks only have to put their initials. There were about five people in yesterday, but no regulars."

"How many were men?" Sadie asked.

"All of them were yesterday. I mean, I can try and give you descriptions, but I don't take all that much notice unless it's someone who comes in regularly. Mind you, there was one guy on terminal seven who has been in a few times over the past week, now that I think about it. He doesn't speak. Or drink coffee," he said with a frown.

Sadie guessed that there was more money in selling fancy coffee than there was in renting out the internet for two dollars an hour.

"We need to get a good look at him," she said. "Do you have a security camera in here?"

"Sure," the Barista said. "If you can just keep an eye on this place, I'll set up the film in the back and then you can go ahead and view it. The way the camera is positioned though, you can't see terminal seven too well."

Sadie thanked him and then turned around to see the three girls watching them, obviously trying to listen to their conversation. The old guy was still deep in Wikipedia.

"What are you girls up to? Talking to boys?" Sadie asked, trying to sound friendly. She remembered being that age, although they didn't have internet cafés then. Instead, she and her friends spent most of their time up at the Lynx lakes, smoking forbidden cigarettes and generally making a nuisance of themselves.

The lakes where Jessica's body had been found. One of the girls at the terminal had long, shiny hair that reminded Sadie of her sister and she felt the familiar ache of a grief that had never really left her. The girls looked fresh and eager, on the very cusp of womanhood, just as Jessica had been before her life had been cruelly snatched away.

"You girls should be careful," Sadie warned when they didn't answer her but looked obviously guilty. "There are a lot of predators out there."

One of the girls rolled her eyes. "You sound like my mom," she said and went back to her screen. So naïve, Sadie thought. They had no idea about the real dangers out there in the world.

The Barista called them through to the back room and Sadie dragged her thoughts back to the matter at hand, following Cooper into the small room, where a screen in the top corner showed the café the day before. The minutes ticked away on the screen. Terminal seven was empty.

"Let me just fast forward a little…there you go," the Barista said. "It's a bit grainy, I'm afraid." He went back out to the coffee bar, leaving Sadie and Cooper to watch the video.

A heavily muffled man, his face shadowed, sat down at terminal seven. The angle of the camera meant that only his feet were visible.

"Okay," Cooper said, leaning forward. "We're at a time when Carmen would have been chatting to her date, and right then there was only Terminal Seven Guy in the café. It's definitely him. Her 'date.'

But we can't see who he is." He cursed loudly. "He must have checked the angle of the camera out and deliberately asked for that terminal."

"Wait," Sadie said and paused the screen. "Look at that."

Cooper frowned. "Look at what, Price?" he asked, sounding confused. "All I can see is a pair of boots."

"Right," Sadie said slowly. "But they aren't just any boots, Sheriff. They're Great White Shark fishing boots with a no-slip tread. Special Edition. They're classics; don't you remember them? They're back in style, but they won't be available everywhere. I bet there are only a few outlets in the whole of Alaska that sell that model."

A slow smile spread across Cooper's face. "Price, you're brilliant," he said, and Sadie was amazed to feel herself blush. "Let's go," he added, making for the door.

"Where are we going, exactly?" Sadie asked.

"Urban Outfitters," the Sheriff said. "The mall just outside of Anchorage center has one…and there isn't anything else like it for miles. If this guy is a local, then the only likely place he has bought those boots is there. And they will have receipts. It's a long shot but…"

"But sometimes long shots pay off," Sadie said, and followed him out of the door.

CHAPTER SEVENTEEN

Surrounded by snow and twinkling with Christmas lights, the Anchorage mall reminded Sadie of a Christmas movie she had watched with Jessica one year. She couldn't remember the plot, other than that it had featured a mean Santa Claus impersonator at a mall and a shy elf. Jessica had found it hilarious.

The memory made her sad and she shook it off, telling herself to concentrate on the matter at hand. When this was all over, then she could take the time to get to the bottom of whatever it was that her father knew about her sister's death.

She had been waiting years; she could wait a little longer.

The Urban Outfitters was one of the biggest stores inside the mall, with large posters announcing the upcoming January sale. As they walked past the various stores, busy shoppers watched Sadie and the Sheriff curiously.

"It's getting late," Cooper said, "You would think people would be getting home for the evening. I've never understood the appeal of malls."

Sadie laughed. "I've never been much of a shopper myself," she admitted.

They entered the busy store to curious stares, and Sadie saw the sales manager approaching them, a wide grin on his face. She frowned, wondering why he seemed so happy to see them.

"Sadie Price?" he said. Sadie searched his face, trying to place it to her memory. He was a tall, red-haired guy with a ponytail and hipster beard, and it took her a moment to remember the chubby, freckled kid that had sat beside her in Math class.

"Toby," she smiled as his name came to mind. "How are you?"

Sadie had encountered a few familiar faces since her return to Anchorage, and mostly those encounters had been neutral at best and unpleasant at worst, but she felt pleased to see Toby. She remembered him as a slightly shy but kind-hearted kid who had once shared his lunch with her when she had no money to get herself a school dinner and had been too embarrassed to ask.

"Really good," Toby grinned. "I manage this place now. I never expected to see you back, but you have clearly done well for yourself. You said that you wanted to be a cop; I knew you would do it."

"Thank you," Sadie said softly. "You've done well too. Manager, hey?"

She was about to explain why they were there, but Toby clearly wanted to talk. He was staring at Sadie with admiration and even, she realized, feeling her cheeks go hot, with attraction. He had always had a bit of a crush on her at school.

Back then, it had never been reciprocated, but time had been good to Toby and Sadie had to admit that he looked good.

Very good, in fact.

"You weren't the only one to get out of here," he told her. "Joey from Chemistry class moved to Canada a few years ago with a Native girl, and the Millett twins went to New York. And about half of our senior high year left for college and never came back."

Sadie shrugged. "It's that kind of place," she acknowledged. "You stayed though; it must have had its charms."

Toby smiled and his dark green eyes crinkled at the sides. He really had turned into a handsome guy, and Sadie felt almost like an awkward teenager again. Especially when he added a wink to go along with that killer smile and she thought about how easily her comment could be construed as flirting. It didn't help either that she could feel Cooper staring at her, the disapproval practically radiating from him.

"This place is like the Titanic," Toby said. "Going down like a sinking ship while everybody races for the lifeboats. What made you come back?"

"The FBI," Sadie said. "I was offered a role here and decided it was time to come home." Which wasn't entirely a lie, she thought, so much as an omission of the whole truth.

The Sheriff cleared his throat loudly. "Speaking of which, Agent, maybe we should get on with why we're here?"

"Right, of course," Sadie said, feeling uncharacteristically flustered. Cooper was standing very stiff, as though someone had shoved a poker up his ass, and she knew that meant that he was pissed off.

Because she was holding them up or because she had appeared to be flirting with Toby?

Toby looked amused as Sadie described to him the boots that they were looking for. He kept glancing from her to the Sheriff, his eyes narrowed as though he was figuring something out.

"Sure," he said when Sadie had finished her description. "We have them in stock. It's a popular brand, but that model is limited edition; otherwise we would be talking thousands of pairs sold. As it is, there have still been hundreds."

"Can you remember selling any recently?" the Sheriff asked, still with a sour expression on his face. "Anything stand out to you about any of the buyers?"

Toby shook his head, looking bemused.

"No. Not that I can think of. I'm sorry that I can't be any more help."

Sadie felt deflated. As she had told Cooper, it was a long shot, but she had still hoped something useful would come of it. She gave Toby a smile that she hoped was the right side of friendly.

"You must have sales receipts for each purchase. It would be useful if we could have them, just in case there is anything that might turn out to be relevant to our investigations."

Toby hesitated. "That could take a few hours Sadie. When do you need them?"

"Tonight?" Sadie suggested. Beside her, Cooper was silent, somehow managing to still radiate disapproval. His eyes were on Toby, with an expression that said he was sizing the other man up.

Toby groaned. "I was hoping for a beer and to watch the hockey game tonight. Is it really that important?"

"Yes," Sadie said. She tipped her head to one side and looked up at him beneath her eyelashes. "It is. But if official police business doesn't move you, how about doing it for old times' sake?"

Toby laughed again, his easy chuckle reminding Sadie of the boy she had known. "I never could say no to you, Sadie Price. All right, I'll do it. The shop shuts at six. Give me your number, and I'll let you know as soon as I'm done."

Sadie gave him her number and they left the shop with Cooper stalking ahead. Sadie avoided looking back at Toby, but she was certain that she could feel him watching her go.

As they got back into the snowcat, Cooper started the engine and pulled off without saying a word.

"All right Cooper," Sadie challenged as they drove away from the mall. "What is your problem?"

"What makes you think I have a problem?" Cooper said, only to follow up straight away with, "Other than you flirting with that guy in there instead of questioning him properly. Another of your ex-boyfriends?"

Sadie winced at the reminder of the first case that they had worked together. "That wasn't very fair," she said. "And what business is it of yours anyway? I persuaded him to get the receipts to us tonight, which is what we need, right? I really don't understand what your problem is here?"

Cooper's usually full mouth was pressed together in a firm line. "It doesn't look professional," he said. "And it could jeopardize the case if he is trying to impress you."

"How?" she challenged.

For a moment, seemingly lost for words, Cooper didn't answer.

"He could pretend there is something useful on the receipts when there isn't; I don't know," he mumbled. "It just isn't professional."

"He wouldn't know what is or isn't useful to us," Sadie pointed out. "This is BS, Cooper. If I didn't know better, I would think you were jealous."

It was Cooper's turn to go red. "Now that," he snapped, "is what is BS."

They didn't speak to each other for the rest of the drive back to the station.

CHAPTER EIGHTEEN

Sadie walked into the saloon, feeling slightly guilty that it was her second social visit in as many days. It was still before eight pm, and the thought of sitting alone in her motel room with hours to kill before bedtime, and nothing to do but think, didn't appeal.

Cooper hadn't spoken to her again after dropping her at the station, other than a curt 'see you in the morning' before he had stomped off into the Station House and she had got into her snow truck. Sadie didn't know what to make of his weird mood. She had been half joking when she had accused him of being jealous, but it did seem to be the only reasonable explanation.

But Cooper, jealous, of her? The thought of him being attracted to her was unnerving. It didn't bode well for a good working relationship.

Not at all.

Yet, Sadie couldn't help grinning to herself at the thought. As stubborn and grumpy as he could be, Logan Cooper was a good guy… and not bad to look at, either.

"What is that little smirk all about?" Caz asked as Sadie approached the bar. The bar owner was already pouring Sadie a whiskey, and the possibility of a non-alcoholic drink that Sadie had been toying with was cast to the wind. A whiskey it was. "You look like the cat that ate the canary. Catch any bad guys?"

"No," Sadie sighed. "It's actually been a rough day. I was just…thinking about something the Sheriff said." She hoped that Caz would leave it there, but the other woman leaned over the bar, resting on her tattooed forearms, and eyed Sadie curiously. Sadie sipped her drink, not meeting the other woman's gaze.

"Ask you out on a date, did he?"

"What? No, of course not!" Sadie nearly coughed on her drink as it burned its way down her throat. "There's nothing between me and the Sheriff. I told you; he's just a colleague."

And that was the truth of it, she told herself firmly. Whatever Cooper's mood had been about, he would snap out of it. The last thing that she needed was to start complicating their professional relationship.

"Mmm hmmm." Making a sarcastic noise through closed lips, Caz looked as though she didn't believe a word. Ignoring her knowing look, Sadie took a gulp of her drink and tried to change the subject.

"Don't mind me; I'm too jaded and too busy for a guy. I spend my time chasing down murderers, not men. But what about you; any dates on the horizon?"

Caz started cleaning a glass, a tired expression on her face that suddenly made her look a lot older than usual. Sadie guessed that the bartender was somewhere in her mid-thirties, just a few years older than Sadie, although the harsh Alaskan winters and lifestyle made many of the locals look older than their years.

"I'm sorry," Sadie said. "I guess that's a touchy subject?"

Caz shrugged her strong shoulders. Although slightly butch, with her short hair, tattoos, and a penchant for shirts and cargo pants, she had a surprisingly fine-boned and pretty face, which her tomboy look highlighted rather than diminished.

"I'm divorced," she said, and there was a heaviness to her voice, as though it made her weary just to think about it. "Married young, fresh out of senior high. That is enough reason to not get married again, you can believe that! Unless," she joked, her face brightening, "the Sheriff is on the market for a ring. I mean, if you don't want him…"

Sadie laughed with her, taking another swig of her drink to quell the prickling of anxiety in the pit of her gut. This wasn't the time to start questioning her feelings for the Sheriff, who half of the time she found completely exasperating.

"I did just bump into an old crush from school," she said, as much to change the subject as out of any desire to talk about Toby, but Caz jumped on this new topic of gossip straight away.

"Tell me more," she said, setting down the glass that she was cleaning and leaning forward on the bar. Sadie felt suddenly self-conscious. Girly chats about guys were something she hadn't indulged in since her college days. It felt nice though; to talk to Caz as though she was a friend rather than the local Fed. Friends had been in short supply in Sadie's life of late.

"It's nothing, really," she said, attempting to backtrack. "I was at the mall – as part of an investigation – and the guy we needed to speak to turned out to be an old school friend."

"Let me guess," Caz said with a wink, "he's turned out kinda cute, huh?"

"Yeah," Sadie smiled, "I guess he has." The whiskey was spreading a warm sensation through her body, relaxing her. How long was it since she had been able to relax and laugh? She was about to order another whiskey when her phone rang.

"Sadie? It's Toby from Urban Outfitters."

"Hey, I was just talking about you," Sadie said before she could stop herself. She felt her face grow hot and Caz, seeing her blush, mouthed 'who is it?' at her.

"Really? Only good things, I hope," Toby said in a low drawl that was surprisingly sexy. He was nothing like the class nerd that she remembered.

Inwardly cringing now, Sadie didn't reply. After a moment's silence, Toby cleared his throat.

"Anyway, I was calling to say that I stayed behind and sorted those receipts out for you. There are quite a few, but if you wanted to swing by and pick them up, I can wait."

Sadie hesitated for a second, thinking of Cooper. Wondering if he would be further annoyed if she picked up the receipts now or waited until they were on the investigation together again in the morning. There wasn't much that she could realistically do with the receipts tonight, and Cooper hadn't been impressed when she had taken it upon it herself to go back to the harbor either.

But then, Sadie reminded herself, she didn't answer to Logan Cooper.

"I'll be there in forty minutes," she told Toby, and ended the call before he could reply.

Caz raised her eyebrows. "I take it that was the guy from the mall?"

"It was," Sadie said without elaborating. She picked up her coat and was shrugging it on when a young woman entered the bar with a girl of around seven years old in tow. The woman looked as though she could be Latina or similar, whereas the girl had short blonde hair and pale skin, and Sadie felt the hairs on the back of her neck rise.

"It's a bit late for a kid to be in a bar," she murmured, more to herself than to Caz, but the bartender raised her eyebrows at Sadie.

"Not when that kid's mom owns the bar," Caz said. Sadie watched in surprise as the girl ran over and ran behind the bar to throw her arms around Caz. "Hi Mommy," she said. "Emily took me to watch the skating. Can I have some chips?"

Sadie looked on as Caz cuddled the girl, whose name was Jenny, supplied the chips, and then let her and Emily through the door at the back of the bar that led upstairs to the living quarters. When Caz turned back to Sadie, there was a softness in her expression that Sadie hadn't seen in her before. She obviously doted on her daughter.

"I had no idea that you had a kid," Sadie said. "She's a little cutie."

"Isn't she just?" Caz said with an indulgent smile. "I try to keep her out of the bar as much as possible, but it's not always easy on my own. I employed Emily as an au pair last year and honestly, the girl has been a Godsend. Jenny absolutely adores her."

Sadie felt her chest tighten in fear. She didn't recognize Caz's daughter from the pictures, but the knowledge of the local case made her draw immediate parallels. She wanted to warn the bartender, but what could she say without spilling details of a case that they were trying to keep as under wraps as possible? Without any indication that Emily had anything to do with the pornography ring, she couldn't panic Caz into thinking that her daughter was in danger.

It might not just be Jenny that could be in danger either, she thought.

"Where's Emily from?" she asked casually.

"Paraguay," Caz said. Sadie felt a stab of relief, although she knew that it could be misguided; there was nothing so far to suggest that the two victims being Filipina was significant in any way.

Sadie went to turn away to leave but then turned back, mentioning to Caz to lean in.

"Keep this to yourself," she said softly, "But keep an eye on Emily. There have been a few au pairs go missing around here just recently. Tell her to be careful if she's dating." That was all she could say; she hoped that it would be enough.

"Oh, but she wouldn't, she's a good girl. And she has a boyfriend back home."

"Okay. Well, I'll see you soon." Sadie smiled as she left, although she still felt uneasy. It was a feeling that stayed with her as she drove back to the mall.

CHAPTER NINETEEN

Sadie spotted Toby leaning against the counter as she walked into the now quiet and empty store. He was waiting for her, and he watched her approach, his eyes admiring. She almost wished that she had stopped to put some lip gloss on and touch herself up a little, but the look in Toby's eyes suggested that he thought she was just fine as she was.

"We meet again," he smiled. "And this time I have something for you."

The innuendo in his voice was subtle – he didn't come across as a sleaze – but it was there. Sadie swallowed, feeling as anxious as a schoolgirl. Was she really this out of practice when it came to men?

"You said you have the receipts?" she said briskly, ignoring his flirting. He looked disappointed, straightening up and reaching behind the counter for a large envelope stuffed with receipts.

"There's quite a few there," he warned her, "But there's only been six in the past two weeks, if that helps."

"It could do," Sadie said cautiously. The boots in the security camera clip had looked new, but it was impossible to guess how new. "But this is great. Thank you for getting them to me so quickly; I really appreciate it."

She had her hand out for the envelope, but Toby lifted it out of the way, a playful look on his face.

"I'll swap them," he teased, "if you let me take you out for dinner some time."

Sadie laughed, shaking her head.

"I'm in the middle of a pretty difficult case, Toby," she told him. "I really don't have the time for a date right now."

"When it's all over then?" he persisted. "We can celebrate you cracking it."

"*If* I crack it," Sadie corrected. Toby still had the envelope held out of her reach. "I'll think about it," she relented.

"Good enough," Toby said with a shrug, handing her the envelope. Sadie took it with a smile, thinking, *what the hell?* One dinner couldn't hurt, especially with someone who had nothing to do with this case or her job in general.

Toby's expression was more serious as he watched Sadie put the envelope into her backpack. "I always liked you at school, Sadie, you know?"

Sadie smiled, feeling touched, their shared history creating a comfortable bond. Laughing with Toby was easy, and uncomplicated.

At least, until his next words, which robbed Sadie of her smile.

"I've always wanted to tell you how bad I felt, you know? About Jessica. It was so awful, what happened to her. I know how close you two were."

Sadie smiled tightly, robbed of an answer as his words felt like a sucker punch to the tentative feelings of desire. Because now when she looked into his eyes, she wasn't just seeing attraction, or simple nostalgia for their schoolyard days.

She saw pity.

"It was a long time ago," she said brusquely, swinging her bag over her shoulder and knowing that the moment was gone. This was the worst thing about returning, after all these years, to Alaska: the people who remembered her sister. Who still gave her the same pitying looks that she had been subjected to over a decade ago.

Even to someone like Toby, Sadie would always be the girl whose sister was murdered. The girl with the alcoholic father.

The girl who had run away.

"I'll see you around, Toby," she said, walking away, but not before she saw the disappointment in his eyes as he sensed her shutting down.

"Remember that dinner?" he called after her.

But Sadie left the store without replying.

*

Back in the dingey motel room, Sadie sat looking through the receipts that Toby had given her. Nothing was out of place about any of the transactions, but then she hadn't expected there to be, not really.

They needed to match the receipts to credit card details, which was going to take some time, not the least because they would need warrants to access the financial details of members of the public. With a serial killer on the loose though, that might not be too difficult. Sadie wondered if it was time that they started feeding details of the murders to the press. They wouldn't be able to keep everything under wraps for long, and the details of the deaths were lurid enough without letting the public imagination get to work on them. The more urgent this case seemed though, the greater the likelihood that they could access the information that they needed.

And it was urgent, she reminded herself. Only two bodies, but they had all the indications of the beginnings of a slew of similar murders. Of a serial killer with a very particular modus operandi. She cringed inwardly as she remembered the state of the bodies.

There was little doubt in Sadie's mind now that a serial killer was exactly what they were looking at, even if logically that didn't seem to fit. Two bodies, and of women who looked similar and were killed in the same way, potentially by a guy posing as an internet date. With the cutting out of the tongues as trophies, it was a textbook case.

The crabs though, Sadie had to admit that was novel, even for her. Whatever happened, this wasn't a case that Sadie would forget in a hurry, no matter how much she might want to. In spite of the features that she would expect from a serial, she was struggling to get inside this killer's head. Sadie wondered if she was losing her touch. Two serial cases one after the other, a child pornography case on the periphery and her own personal issues... it was all enough to fry anyone's brain.

The fact that the victims might be implicated in the child pornography case too, was a distraction that Sadie didn't need. Not just because it wasn't clear how the cases were linked, even if it was becoming apparent that there was a link somewhere, but because it complicated Sadie's feelings for the victims themselves. She wasn't naïve enough to believe that there were only two types of people in the world, the bad guys and the good guys. She knew that people were more complex than that. That, given the right circumstances, we all had a mix of both the sinner and the saint. Murder victims didn't have to be angels to deserve justice.

But child pornography? That was a unique evil that Sadie couldn't get her thoughts around. In no way did either of the victims, assuming they were guilty, deserve anything that had happened to them, but it certainly made Sadie think about just what could push a parent over the edge when it came to protecting their kids.

The notion of justice felt significant. She intuitively felt that this killer was driven by more than just a sick fetish for killing women, of whatever occupation. This was someone trying to right a wrong – but one done to him, or to someone else?

To his child, perhaps?

Pushing the receipts away from her, she stood up, pacing back and forth across the small room as she tried to get her thoughts into some form of coherent order. She was exhausted, her limbs heavy with fatigue, yet also wired at the same time, the events of the day a mass of jumbled images in her mind's eye.

She could well imagine a parent snapping who had discovered their au pair was taking abusive images of their child and taking their revenge too far, but that didn't explain both bodies. Unless the parents had got together?

No, Sadie thought, her instincts told her that this was a lone killer. It was the tongues; it felt too personal. A parent group wanting revenge wouldn't do that. Not so cleanly and clinically, anyway.

Unless one of the parents already had psychopathic tendencies? This could be just the push they needed...and maybe after one murder, they found that they just couldn't stop. It was a common enough scenario, with many serial killers promising themselves that the first one would be the last. But one killing was never enough to feed the beast.

Sadie thought about Mr. Randolph, who not only had a motive but also knew about boats.

Sighing, she stopped midway across the room and rubbed her now stinging eyes, admitting defeat. It would all have to wait until morning.

She undressed and got into bed, hoping that she wouldn't lie awake in the dark, alone with her own morbid thoughts.

She didn't. Sleep overtook her as soon as her head touched the pillow, which would have been a relief to her tired mind and aching body if the dream hadn't followed soon after.

It started the way that they always did, with a teenage Sadie running down the snow-covered hill in her night gown, calling after her sister. Calling for her to come back. Sometimes in these dreams Jessica was being pulled along by a man whose features Sadie couldn't make out, but sometimes she was alone, like now. Walking away from Sadie without turning around, either unable to hear or ignoring her sister's calls.

"Jessica! Come back. Don't go near the lake!" Sadie screamed, but the wind snatched her voice. Jessica walked on ahead, her hair streaming out in the wind. She was a ghost, her outline fuzzy, her body translucent, but instead of fading away as she usually did Jessica carried on walking, right out onto the frozen lake. Sadie ran after her, sobbing. She was so cold that her teeth were chattering, and her hands and feet were numb, but she kept running even though she had to force her legs to move.

She gasped when her feet touched the frozen water on the surface of the lake, whimpering at the pain. But she kept on, following Jessica as her sister made her way out into the middle of the lake where the ice would be thinnest.

Then suddenly, her sister disappeared.

"Jessica!" Sadie screamed, howling in despair.

Then she heard her, just a faint whimper, pleading for help, but she couldn't see her. Sadie spun on the ice, looking around her frantically, but there was no sign of Jessica anywhere. Until Sadie saw a dark shape underneath her now frozen feet, floating underneath the ice.

Jessica. Sadie fell to her hands and knees, clawing frantically at the ice, hammering at it with her fists to make the ice crack underneath her so that she could pull her sister to safety. Could save her. She could just make out her sister's features underneath the ice, her eyes wide with fear. Her lips moved, framing words that spurred Sadie on in her furious digging even as she knew it was useless.

"Help me, Sadie,"

Sadie sobbed as she continued to claw at the surface of the lake, and her tears froze on her cheek.

"Hold on, Jessica, hold on," she pleaded even as her sister began to sink further down into the lake, falling out of sight. Sadie clasped her hands together and hammered frantically with her joined fists until finally, the ice began to crack. Sadie sobbed with relief as Jessica floated back up towards her.

Then she stared in horror as she realized that something was very wrong with her sister's face. She swam into view, and Sadie scuttled back, retching.

A crab's claw was hanging from her sister's hair, and her face was half rotted away. No, not rotted...eaten. Bone showed through her flesh.

Sadie screamed.

When she woke up, bolting upright in her bed in the dark room, she was still screaming.

CHAPTER TWENTY

The Trooper on the desk gave Sadie a concerned look as she walked in.

"I know, I look like shit," Sadie said before the guy could comment. "Bad night." She made her way to the Sheriff's office, smoothing her braid down as she went. There had been nothing that she could do about the bags under her eyes or the gray pallor to her skin, other than gulp three mugs of coffee one after the other, which had only had the effect of making her look frazzled.

Cooper didn't seem to notice her appearance though, glancing up at her and then frowning at the envelope that she was holding out.

"Toby called last night. I picked the receipts up," she told him, expecting him to look pleased. Instead, he took them from her with a look of distaste.

"Something up, Cooper?" Sadie snapped. "I didn't just wipe my ass with the envelope."

The Sheriff sat back in his chair, his eyebrows flying up his forehead at Sadie's uncharacteristic rudeness. Sadie sank into the chair opposite him.

"I'm sorry," she said, pressing her head into her hand. "I had a bad night's sleep and drank way too much coffee this morning. I feel like some kind of goddamn zombie."

"If you need to take a break, Price," Cooper offered, "I can manage today. I'll call you if there are any major developments."

Sadie shook her head and tried to laugh, although it came out sounding brittle. "You're not getting rid of me that easily," she protested. "I'll be fine."

"Okay," Cooper said, and Sadie felt relieved that he had decided not to push his suggestion, "Well, I spoke to Carmen's agent this morning. Harvey Silverman. He runs the biggest au pair agency for miles, operates in a few other cities although the base is in Anchorage. I've met him once: slimy kinda guy."

Sadie's ears pricked up. A new lead meant something concrete to get her teeth into, which she felt would perk her up more than Cooper's offer of a break. She would only spend it pacing her motel room again.

"Did he know she had disappeared?"

"I haven't asked him yet. I thought we could do it face-to-face this morning. But I did find out the name of the other missing au pair, the one that the kids have fingered as grooming them into posing for those pictures."

Sadie nodded. "Go on."

"Dana Ramos. Latino stepfather, but her parents are Filipino, just like Carmen's, although that might not be significant. Silverman gets a lot of his employees from the Philippines."

He let his comment hang in the air, waiting for Sadie to pick up on it.

"Dana was also employed by Silverman's agency?"

"Yep," Cooper confirmed. "Not only that, but the family had reported Dana's disappearance to Harvey, assuming that she had run off. But there is no record of anyone at the agency reporting it to the police."

Sadie whistled under her breath.

"He knows something," she said.

"Without a doubt," Cooper replied. "And Silverman strikes me as a more likely candidate to be heading up a potential international pornography ring than someone like Higgins."

"So, we're back to our original theory," Sadie said. "The girls were threatening to squeal, or perhaps simply bail and Silverman had them killed? He wouldn't be silly enough to be the guy at terminal seven – although there could be more than one person involved."

Cooper watched her face for a few moments. "You're still not convinced," he said matter-of-factly. "You still think we're looking at the next serial killer?"

"Maybe that's just become my norm," Sadie sighed, "But yes. It may not be the most obvious conclusion right now, but it's one I just can't seem to shake." *And I was right on the last one*, she thought. Both the Sheriff and Deputy Cooper had tried to reason her out of her conclusions then, too.

"Perhaps Silverman – or whoever – wanted to make it deliberately look that way? To throw us off the scent?" Cooper suggested. Sadie looked doubtful.

"But then why the elaborate show, in that case? He could just have killed and then dumped them quietly. The families might not even have ever reported them missing, but just continued to think that they had gone home. It's just like the thing with the crabs. He wants them to suffer, to be mutilated. It isn't just a way of getting rid of the bodies, because he doesn't kill them first. And if he is connected to the harbor – which he must be, to have that sort of access – then he would know there was no way that the bodies would go unnoticed. He's taking risks, because he thinks that he's too smart to get caught – or he doesn't care if he is. Killers like this want to be noticed."

Cooper gave her a long look, and then nodded slowly. "I can see your logic, Price, even if this isn't my area," he said. "This whole case is so tangled. Nothing is straightforward about it. But, if we keep on chipping away at all these different angles, we'll get there."

Sadie stood up. "I hope you're right. So, I guess that going to see Silverman is next on our list?"

Cooper stood up, noticing as he did so that the envelope full of receipts was still in his hand. He locked it into a drawer, and then hesitated before asking her, "So, you saw Toby again last night?" His eyes were looking everywhere but at Sadie.

So *that* explained the face he had pulled when he had taken the receipts from her.

"Yes, I said that already," Sadie said without elaborating any further. It was none of Cooper's damn business that Toby had asked her to go for dinner with him, and neither did she want to explain her reasons for turning the sales manager down.

"Right," Cooper said, pursing his lips and leaving the office without another word. Sadie followed him, wondering just when the source of tension between the Sheriff and her had changed so much.

*

As they drove, Sadie wanted to talk about this new development in the case, but Cooper was quiet, answering her in grunts. She wondered if he was still pissed at her over Toby and was about to just outright ask him when Cooper spoke, surprising her with his words.

"I know this might not be a good time to bring this up, Price," he began, "But I've been thinking about what you asked me."

Sadie frowned, wondering what he was talking about "What did I ask you?"

"About your sister."

Sadie leaned her head against the window, remembering a few nights ago, at the harbor when they had been sitting in the truck together, keeping watch. Before they had seen Higgins going into the Bait Shack and everything had started happening at a speed too fast to think about much else.

She had asked him about her sister's case, and whether he had ever looked at it. If he knew anything.

At the mention of Jessica, last night's dream swam back into the forefront of her consciousness and Sadie blinked her eyes against it as though she could somehow prevent herself from seeing the images her mind had conjured up.

The bad dreams had always been with her, surfacing more often at times of stress, but since coming back to Alaska, they were recurring every few nights. Leaving her waking in the morning drenched in an icy sweat and with hot tears on her cheeks. It was one of the reasons that Caz's whiskey was starting to look so appealing.

"I remember," she said, and waited for Cooper to speak.

"I had a look at the files last night," he told her. "I wanted to see if I could find out anything for you, and I guess I needed a distraction from all this. Bottom line is, whoever was on your sister's case back then was hardly the Alaskan State Trooper's brightest and best. There were things that were missed, or just not followed up on."

Sadie sucked in her breath at this news. It was something that she had long suspected, but to hear her suspicions validated was as unnerving as it was an impetus for her to discover more. She tried not to seem too eager as she replied, but her words came out in a rush.

"Like what, Cooper?"

Cooper seemed to hesitate. "Persons of interest who were never re-interviewed, that sort of thing."

Sadie stared at his profile. His eyes were fixed on the road ahead, but she saw him swallow, and saw the slight twitch at the corner of his mouth.

"Cooper," she said in a low voice. "Spit it out. What is it that you're not telling me?"

There was a pause before Cooper answered, during which whatever he was about to say seemed to weigh, tangibly, in the air between them. Sadie shifted in her seat.

"Cooper?" She was almost pleading with him now.

The Sheriff cleared his throat. “Okay,” he said. “As an example – probably the most significant – when your father called 911 to report Jessica missing, that isn’t quite what he reported, if you know what I mean.”

“No,” Sadie snapped, running out of patience, “I don’t know what you mean.”

“His exact words – you can hear them quite clearly on the audio, even though there’s some crackling – is ‘they took her.’ He sounds panicked. But later on, after her body was found, he denied ever saying it, and it was never followed up. He was never pushed on it. Perhaps they thought that he had been drunk when he called...but even so. I would have followed that up, if only to rule the possibility of kidnapping out.”

Sadie was sitting up straight now, watching the frozen landscape roll by without taking in any of it. She was trying to absorb Cooper’s words, to make sense of what they meant.

Of what they implied.

That Jessica had been taken. Had been murdered, just as Sadie had always thought, even when everyone had told her to drop it, that it was an accident, and the grief was just driving her crazy. But she had always known that she wasn’t crazy.

This confirmed it.

It also confirmed what she had recently been told: that her father knew something about it.

They took her.

“Who?” she said aloud, although she was talking to herself rather than the Sheriff. “Who took her?”

The question hung in the air, and a loaded silence settled over the interior of the snowcat.

“If you like, when we’ve caught this bastard,” Cooper said eventually, “maybe we could look into it. Together.”

Sadie jerked round in her seat, staring at Cooper. “Really? You would do that? But why?”

Cooper was still staring fixedly at the road, and he gave a small shrug, as though it was no big deal, but Sadie saw the high spots of pink on his cheekbones. He knew exactly what this would mean to her, and she had a sudden urge to hug him.

She didn’t, of course.

“I’ve always liked the idea of taking on a cold case,” Cooper said. “And this one...it makes me embarrassed that my predecessors did such a lame job on it. It's an injustice. Jessica deserved better...and so do you."

"Thank you," Sadie whispered. There was another pause, during which she wrestled inwardly with a tide of conflicting emotion. Anger, at her father and the cops who had bungled her sister's case, but also elation that Cooper was prepared to open it back up and, more than that, to help her.

On top of that was the fear of what she might find.

Especially if it turned out that her father had been involved. Or had known something and kept it quiet all these years. Jessica had been the one that he was fond of, the one that he loved, in as much as her father was capable of loving anyone. It made no sense to Sadie, at least on the surface.

Underneath though, a darker part of her that was only too aware of the evil that people could do even to the ones they loved, wondered if she was really all that shocked. If at some barely conscious level, she had expected this all along. If her years at the BAU had taught her anything, it was that people were always capable of worse than was expected of them.

It wasn't a field that lent itself to a rosy perception of human nature.

"It means I'll have to question you as well," Cooper said, breaking through her dark thoughts. "Go through your own memories of the morning that she disappeared. It might be upsetting for you, but it's important this gets done right...this time."

Sadie nodded. It was what she would do, too. "It's fine," she said. "It isn't exactly a memory that I've buried. It's become crystallized in my mind like amber, in fact. I just wish there was something different to tell. I've been over and over it in my own head so many times over the years, but nothing ever stands out. We all went to bed as usual, and in the morning, she had gone. We searched for her day and night and then the next day, she was found in the lake. People wondered if she had killed herself, but there was no way...nothing had changed, she wasn't sad."

Plus, Sadie knew that there was no way that Jessica would leave her little sister alone with their father, but she didn't tell Cooper that. She didn't feel ready to discuss their family dynamics with the Sheriff, although eventually she would need to, if he was going to investigate Jessica's death.

He would need to speak to her father, too.

"Going over it with someone new might jog something loose," Cooper suggested. "It does happen. Do you have any gut feeling about who your father might have been talking about on that call?"

They took her. "None," Sadie said, sounding frustrated. She shook her head. "If I had known about that, I would have left no stone unturned. I can't believe whoever was investigating just left it. They didn't even ask me about it. I was fifteen; I was old enough."

Cooper nodded. "It was a shambles. It almost makes me wonder..."

He bit the words off before he could get them out, but Sadie already knew what he was going to say.

"If it was a cover-up?" She finished his sentence for him. "I'm wondering that, too. If there was some reason why it was never pursued. But it's not as though my father was a popular guy with friends on the force, or anything like that."

"We'll look at every angle," Cooper assured her. "If there is anything to find, then we'll find it."

"Thanks, Cooper," Sadie said again before turning her head to stare out of her window. She didn't want Cooper to see the effect that his words were having on her. She felt like crying, both in frustration that this had been kept from her for so long and also, embarrassingly, in gratitude for the promise of the Sheriff's help.

They didn't speak for the rest of the journey, but the atmosphere was less tense. Sadie, though, couldn't help but turn what Cooper had told her over and over in her mind. This wasn't just a forgotten piece of peripheral information; this was a potential bombshell. It was the first tangible piece of evidence she had that her sister's death wasn't what it seemed. Finally, there was something to go on and a trail to follow.

But it was a trail that started with her father, which meant that whether the old man liked it or not, at some point he was going to have to speak to her and answer her questions about the past.

And about that phone call. Which Sadie needed to listen to, herself, as soon as possible.

Because according to Cooper, he hadn't just said 'Someone took her.' He had said 'They took her.' Which could imply only one thing.

That her father knew who 'they' were.

CHAPTER TWENTY ONE

Sadie was still reeling from the new information on her sister's death when they walked into the reception of the agency. She felt brittle and on edge and had to resist snapping impatiently at the blonde receptionist, who looked up at them and then went back to her phone call, taking her time before she replaced the receiver and eyed them suspiciously.

"Can I help you?" she asked, in an accent that wasn't American, but that Sadie couldn't quite place. So far it seemed that Harvey Silverman only employed foreign women. If they couldn't get him on anything else, Sadie suspected that Immigration might be very interested in the Silverman au pair agency.

"Yes," the Sheriff said, flashing his badge. "You can go and get your boss for us please ma'am. We need to ask him a few questions."

The woman looked panicked and bit her lip. "Err, I'm not sure if he is still here," she said, the nerves evident in her voice.

"His car is outside, so I'm sure he is," Sadie said sweetly. The receptionist said nothing, although her eyes widened. She got up and went through a door at the back of the room. They heard low voices, and then the blonde woman was back.

"He will see you now," she said, not meeting their eyes. Sadie noticed that her hands were trembling slightly.

"Good of him," Cooper murmured as they walked into Silverman's office. It was plush, with a thick carpet, heavy oak desk and a huge leather chair. It smelled of men's perfume, covering a faint odor of something musky, a body scent, that made Sadie wrinkle her nose. She wondered just what Silverman and his receptionist had been up to that day.

Silverman himself was tall and heavy set, just the wrong side of stocky, with chunky gold rings on his fingers and a shining, closely shaved head. He gave the impression of someone trying very hard to look like a legitimate businessman but not being quite able to shake off the appearance of a thug. He stood up to shake Cooper's hand and then

Sadie's, giving Cooper a fake smile that showed expensive dental work.

When he looked at Sadie the smile remained, but his eyes flickered downwards, lingering over her body in a way that made Sadie want to cover up, even though she was already bundled up against the cold.

Harvey Silverman was a sleaze.

"Please, sit down," he said, waving them into the chairs opposite his desk. "How can I help you? Nothing that my girls have been up to, I hope?"

His tone was easy and relaxed, but Sadie still picked up on the tension coming from him. There was a sheen of sweat on his brow that certainly wasn't being generated by the temperature.

Not yet wanting to reveal that she was from the FBI, Sadie let Cooper do the initial talking while she watched the agency owner carefully.

"We need to ask you a few details about your employees and their clients, yes. Mr. Silverman. It seems that some of your girls have gone missing recently. Within the past few days, in fact."

Silverman sat back in his chair, steepling his fingers and looking thoughtful. Sadie noticed his right eye twitch. He wasn't as slick as he thought he was; his body language gave him away before he even opened his mouth.

"Nothing has been reported as recently as that, I'm afraid, but it does happen from time to time. The girls meet someone and run off, or they decide that they don't like the job and go back home without bothering to work out their notice." Silverman shrugged. "It's one of the risks of the job. I vet every au pair I take on the books of course and check out their references, but you can't ever be sure. But I'll let you know as soon as I hear anything. Now, if you don't mind, Sheriff, I have a brunch appointment." Silverman started to stand up, indicating that he was ready to see them out.

"Then you had better cancel it, Mr. Silverman," Cooper said pleasantly, "Because we haven't finished."

Silverman looked angry, pausing halfway out of his chair, his hands on his desk so that he was leaning over them. "I'm really not sure how I can help," he snapped. "I've told you…"

"Did you know that Carmen was murdered?" Cooper asked. Silverman sat back down slowly, staring at the Sheriff. Sadie watched him closely.

"Murdered," he said flatly. It was a statement, rather than a question. His small, dark eyes were opaque and devoid of emotion, but his forehead still glistened with sweat. He was nervous, just as the receptionist had been.

"Yes," the Sheriff continued. "Her body was found yesterday morning. The last time that she had been seen was the afternoon before. It appears that she had a date with someone that she met off the internet. Would you know anything about that?"

Silverman looked annoyed at the Sheriff's question. "We're an au pair agency," he said, "Not a dating agency. How would I know about that? I don't keep tabs on them once they've been assigned to a client, not unless there's a complaint."

The Sheriff nodded. "I get that, Mr. Silverman. What I don't understand," he said thoughtfully, "is why you didn't report the fact that Dana Ramos also went missing just a few days before Carmen."

Sadie saw the man flinch at Dana's name. "I told you," he said, "I don't keep tabs on them. Sometimes this just happens."

"*Murder* just happens, Mr. Silverman?" Sadie asked, speaking to him for the first time since he had greeted her. "Because that seems very unlucky, don't you think? Two of your au pairs dead in less than a week?"

"I don't know what you think you're implying," Silverman said, his eyes narrowing, "But if you carry on that way then you're going to need a warrant. I don't need to tell you anything."

Cooper shot Sadie a warning glance. They didn't want Silverman to shut down before they had the chance to find out anything from him.

"It's just a few questions," the Sheriff said smoothly. Silverman glared at him.

"Your sidekick here seems to be accusing me of murder," he snapped. Sadie saw the corners of Cooper's mouth twitch at the word 'sidekick,' as though suppressing a smile, and she had to bite back the retort that was on her lips.

"Actually, I'm a Federal Agent, Mr. Silverman," she said instead. "Special Agent Price, in fact. We're investigating a murder, so if you refuse to comply then a warrant is exactly what I'll be getting. Two of your au pairs have gone missing and bodies matching their descriptions have turned up. Within days of each other, and both in Anchorage. So naturally, we would want to question one of the few links between both of the murdered women."

Silverman stared at her, looking as though he was weighing up his actions. Finally, he went for an apologetic smile, one that didn't reach his eyes.

"This is all a bit of a shock, Agent Price," he said, finally wiping his brow as he spoke. "The last I knew, both Carmen and Dana were happily settled in their new positions."

"That's odd," Sadie went on, "Because the family that Dana was settled with did in fact report her missing, although not to the police. To you."

There was a silence, during which Silverman opened and closed his mouth like a fish. "I…yes, you're right," he said finally. "It slipped my mind; as I said, these things do happen. It was the shock, you see, you coming in here talking about murders."

He was gabbling, and Sadie felt a surge of anger towards the man. He was clearly lying to them now; meanwhile Carmen and Dana lay half-eaten in the morgue.

Carmen and Dana who, it seemed, had been abusing the girls in their care. There was nothing to connect either of them to Higgins as yet, other than the pictures themselves, but they were connected to this man who sat in front of them. Sadie decided to apply the pressure. They had caught Silverman off guard, and he was starting to panic, which meant that he was liable to give something important away.

"I see," she said coolly. "And what about the pictures, Mr. Silverman? Did you forget to mention those, too?"

"What pictures?" he frowned, but Sadie saw the flash of fear in his eyes and knew that he was aware of exactly what she was talking about. She leaned forward as she spoke, her eyes fixed on his, and allowed the utter contempt that she felt for this man to show in her voice.

"There were pictures found of the children in Carmen and Dana's care," she said. "Naked pictures, Mr. Silverman. Of little kids," she spat, feeling her face twist with disgust. Suddenly, it was all too much, and she wanted nothing more than to throttle the man in front of her with her bare hands. He was a piece of shit, and he was wasting their time with his lies.

"Price," Cooper murmured, but Sadie ignored him. Silverman was shaking his head from side to side rapidly.

"Oh, no, you're not pinning this on me," he said quickly. Too quickly. There was no real shock in his face, or disgust, which should surely be the natural reaction to such an accusation.

"So, what happened?" Sadie asked. She regained her composure as she sat back in her chair, but inside her anger remained, burning in her chest like Caz's whiskey. "Did they threaten to squeal, or did you decide that they knew too much? Perhaps they didn't want to do it anymore? You couldn't have them backing out and then wandering around feeling guilty about what they had done, could you?"

Silverman jumped to his feet, aptly reminding her of the way Higgins had raged at them in the shack. "Get out of my office!" he roared.

Cooper got to his feet, too. "We will be back with a warrant, Mr. Silverman," he said. "I suggest that you don't attempt to leave Anchorage without letting us know where you're going."

Sadie got to her feet and followed Cooper out of the office, ignoring Silverman, who was glaring at her hard.

"You will be hearing from my lawyers!" he yelled after them. "This is defamation of character!"

Cooper shut the door behind them and raised an eyebrow at Sadie. "That went well," he said sarcastically.

Sadie ignored him. She was watching the receptionist, who had been talking urgently into the phone when they had emerged from Silverman's office and was now replacing the receiver and looking nervously over at them. Sadie walked over to the reception desk and leaned over it. The phone was in full view.

"Yes?" the blonde woman asked. Sadie smiled at her.

"I don't suppose you have a pen and paper that I could use, please?" she asked. The woman looked taken aback, but then passed her a pen and a notepad. Sadie scribbled the information down that she wanted, tore the paper from the pad and handed the woman her things back before rejoining Cooper, who was looking at her curiously.

As soon as they were in the snowcat, he turned to her, nodding at the piece of paper in her hand.

"What was that all about?" he asked.

"I've got a photographic memory for numbers," Sadie told him. "I wrote down the number of whoever the woman was speaking to when we came out of the office. There was something about the way that she was watching the door as we came out; it just struck me as suspicious."

"Right," Cooper said, looking unconvinced. "Price, I wish you hadn't gone in on Silverman like that. It was too hard, too quick. It will scare him off. I wouldn't be surprised if he disappears. Now he won't talk, and we barely asked him about the murders."

But Sadie wasn't listening. She was too busy phoning the number that she had written down on the piece of paper in her hand.

It went through to voicemail. She listened carefully to the recorded message, then cut the call without leaving a response.

"Nothing?" Cooper said, not sounding surprised.

"Voicemail," Sadie said. "The receptionist must have been leaving a message."

Then she gave a triumphant smile.

"The number belongs to Joe Higgins," she said.

CHAPTER TWENTY TWO

Sadie and Cooper sat opposite Higgins and Erin Curtis, who was less than happy at being called back into the station. Sadie suspected that Curtis had bigger fish to fry; she couldn't imagine that the woman would be in Anchorage defending petty crooks for too long.

"This had better be good, Sheriff," Curtis said, tapping those long fingernails on the table. Next to her, Higgins looked tired and deflated. Two days in a cell here, cold and with only basic amenities, would hopefully have given him time to think about his best course of action.

Cooper ignored the lawyer and addressed Higgins instead. The pictures had been brought out of Evidence again and were laid on the table in front of them. The lawyer was carefully avoiding looking at them. Sadie wondered how she could manage to do it: defend a child pornographer. If she herself had ever gone into law, she knew it would have been as a prosecutor. The thought of defending the likes of Higgins or Silverman turned her stomach.

"We had a chat with your friend today," Cooper said to Higgins, who gave him a surly look.

"What friend?" he asked.

Cooper waited a beat before he dropped the name. "Harvey Silverman," he said. Higgins's eyes went wide, and he looked at Curtis and then back at Cooper. He seemed lost for words.

"Do you know him?" Cooper asked. Higgins shook his head mutely.

"Maybe you could explain, then," Sadie asked, speaking in a casual voice, "why he has your number?"

"I don't know!" Higgins exclaimed, looking as guilty as all hell.

"It seems strange, if you don't know him, that he would have your number," Cooper commented. He looked at Sadie. "Don't you think, Agent Price?"

"Cut the bull crap, you two," Curtis snapped before Sadie could answer. "My client has already informed you that he doesn't know this person. Move on."

Higgins had slumped in his seat again, looking exhausted. If it wasn't for Curtis, Sadie was sure that the bait man would have confessed already. He was no criminal mastermind, and he must know that pleading guilty would get him a lighter sentence than if a jury convicted him. Which, with Guthrie's evidence as well as Sadie finding the pictures, was pretty much a certainty.

"Your client," Cooper said to her, "would be better served by telling us what he knows in the hope of cutting a deal for his information. Unless of course he wants to take the sole responsibility for the child pornography."

"We know it was the au pairs who were taking the pictures, Joe," Sadie told him, continuing the Sheriff's line of inquiry. "The same au pairs that have ended up dead. The same au pairs, in fact, who worked for Silverman, the man that you claim not to know, even though he clearly knows you."

Higgins put his head in his hands and didn't reply. Sadie and the Sheriff waited, while Curtis glared at them but didn't interrupt, waiting to see what unfolded. She must have known by now that her client was screwed, Sadie thought.

Finally, Higgins sat back up, although he remained hunched over at the shoulders. His eyes were wet, Sadie saw, although she couldn't muster up an ounce of sympathy for him. She would save that for the children he had exploited. When she spoke though, she kept her tone soft.

"This is the thing, Joe," she said. "We know that Silverman is at the head of all this, and that he probably killed Dana and Carmen. If you can tell us what you know, it will go well for you in court. There might even be the possibility of cutting a deal. Do you really want to take the rap for a lowlife like Silverman?"

Higgins sighed. He looked at Curtis, who responded with the slightest nod of her chin.

"Okay," he said heavily. "I'll tell you what I know about the pictures. But I swear, I don't know nothin' about no murders. I wouldn't put it past Silverman, but I don't know anything about it. The pictures though, that's just the start of it. Silverman trafficks the women as well as the kids. False papers, none of them are legal. That's how he gets them to do it; he's got their passports."

Sadie felt her heart beating a fast tattoo in her chest and next to her she could feel Cooper tensing up. This was it. They had him.

"Okay," Cooper said slowly. "So, tell us about the kids in the pictures. Where did you come in?"

"I know Silverman from down at the harbor," Higgins said, looking at the floor between his feet as he spoke. "He has one of them fancy yachts. Mostly he keeps it up at the private harbor out of town, but sometimes he docks at the main one. When he does, he buys bait from me. The turkey heads, they're his favorite."

"Right," Sadie said, impatient to get to the information that they needed. "So, how did you get from selling him turkey heads to distributing child pornography for him?"

Higgins shuffled his feet and cleared his throat, a hacking, phlegmy sound that made Sadie inwardly cringe.

"Everyone knows that Silverman has his fingers in a lot of pies," he said. "That you can get stuff from him. Immigration papers, women…and the other stuff. The kiddy stuff." For the first time, Higgins looked ashamed. "I have tried to get help," he whispered, so that Cooper and Sadie had to lean forward to hear him. "After I was arrested before, I went to a treatment program, but…" his words trailed off and he continued staring at his feet.

"You asked Silverman for the pornography," Sadie guessed. "And he saw an opportunity to make a bit more cash?"

Higgins nodded.

"We need you to answer us in words, Joe."

"Yeah," he said bitterly. "He had me, didn't he, once I had asked him? He could have told everyone. Some of the fishermen, they're no better than me, but the others…they would have hurt me if they had known. He said I wouldn't get caught, and that I could make some cash."

"But you recruited Johnny Guthrie, just in case you needed a fall guy," Cooper said. He wasn't falling for Higgins's sob story any more than Sadie was.

"I needed somewhere safe to keep them," Higgins said. "Kids are always stealing things out of the bait shack. I knew Johnny liked collecting things and could be a bit light-fingered, so I knew he must have a hidey-hole. And that he would be too scared to tell anyone. So, I brought him in, but I only gave him a couple of names. DaCosta distributed the rest."

Sadie raised an eyebrow. So DaCosta had been involved after all. Probably a lot more so than Higgins realized, given his record. Higgins was small fry. DaCosta and Silverman had used Higgins as their fall guy, much like Higgins had tried to use Johnny.

"So, there were more fishermen buying the pictures than the two names that Johnny gave us?" Cooper said. Higgins nodded.

"Yeah. At least ten. Out at sea, none of this digital stuff works, you see? Silverman does all that internet crap too, but I had nothing to do with that."

No, I don't see, Sadie thought, turning away so that her thoughts didn't show in her face. How could there be so many twisted people around? People who wouldn't think twice about hurting and abusing little kids? Thinking about just how deep this could go was nauseating her.

"Thank you, Joe," she said briskly, gathering up the folder. "Unless the Sheriff has any more questions for you, I think we're done for now. You'll be getting a date for your bail hearing."

Higgins closed his eyes. His face going slack like putty. He didn't acknowledge them as they left the room. Sadie nodded at Curtis, who looked furious, and Sadie tried not to show her disdain for the woman. She had nothing against lawyers in general but drew the line when it came to anyone willing to represent – to defend - scum like Higgins.

Outside the room, Cooper was bouncing on his heels with excitement, and the eager look on his face almost made Sadie laugh, brightening her dark mood. She knew how much this meant to him.

The victims were local kids.

"We'll pick the Deputy up on the way. Let's go and get our guy," he said, and Sadie followed him out, content in this instance to let the Sheriff take the lead.

*

Sadie's heart was thumping fast in her chest as they jumped down from the snowcat and entered the agency. She had been expecting to find Silverman gone, but his car was thankfully still outside.

The receptionist's mouth fell open as she saw them, and she immediately jumped to her feet. "I'll tell you anything you need to know," she gasped, tears springing to her eyes. "I never wanted to be involved. He made me. My sister…she works for him too." The woman burst into tears and Jane exchanged a look with Sadie and the Sheriff.

"We'll need a statement later," she murmured. The Sheriff nodded and walked swiftly towards Silverman's office with Sadie close behind.

He didn't bother to knock.

Inside, Silverman was hurriedly thrusting his laptop into a bag, a window wide open behind him. It was big enough to climb out of.

"Going somewhere?" Sadie said sweetly as the man made a dash for the window and then froze as Cooper pulled out his gun.

"Step away from the window, put the bag down and put your hands up," Cooper ordered, his voice a low growl. Silverman looked from one to the other, his piggy little eyes calculating as he weighed up his options.

"You have until the count of three," Cooper said. He was speaking through gritted teeth, and Sadie suspected that if he ended up having to shoot Silverman, it wouldn't exactly ruin his day.

She knew that feeling, and the naked hatred in Cooper's eyes brought back uncomfortable memories.

"Logan," she said softly, but Silverman had already made up his mind. He moved back behind his desk and placed his bag back on top of it. Sadie hoped that he hadn't manage to wipe all his files before they had returned but judging by the fact that he was still here, she guessed that he either hadn't known that Higgins was in custody or hadn't expected him to fold so soon.

"Move to the side of your desk so I can see your whole body," Cooper ordered. "And put your hands up. I won't tell you again, Silverman."

Silverman did as he was commanded, and although there was a smirk on his face, Sadie could see the worry in his eyes. He had to be wondering just how much they knew, and how much evidence they had against him. He was sweating again, and his suit had damp patches under the armpits.

"I hope you have a good explanation for this, Sheriff," Silverman said, still trying to keep up his façade of outraged innocence. Sadie grinned at him.

"We have a very good explanation, Mr. Silverman. One so good that you're going to accompany us to the Station so that we can explain it to you."

Silverman looked at her as though he wanted to throttle her. "Do I have any choice in the matter, Agent?" he snapped.

"No," Cooper answered for her. "You don't. Harvey Silverman, we're arresting you on charges of making and distributing child pornography, human trafficking, and murder. You might want to think about a lawyer."

Silverman's face drained of color. He didn't speak or attempt to resist as Sadie cuffed him, walking silently out of the office with his hands raised and Cooper's gun at his back.

Sadie glanced at Cooper and smiled to see the wide, satisfied grin on his face.

CHAPTER TWENTY THREE

Sadie replaced her phone in her pocket with Golightly's praise still ringing in her ears.

"Good work once again, Agent Price. You're proving to be quite the asset," he had told her. Sadie had held her breath in horror, worrying that Golightly was about to put her in charge of the whole case, but thankfully, he hadn't. Child pornography wasn't her area, and she had no intention of making it so.

The blonde receptionist had also agreed to testify immediately. Silverman's criminal enterprise was falling down like a house of cards. With growing evidence that the whole thing was wider than just Alaska, the case would pass from State hands into those of the FBI, and Golightly would already be on the phone to the Field Agencies in the other states that Silverman operated in.

They had left Silverman to fester in a cell for a while as they went over Higgins's statement and the Deputy questioned the receptionist, whose name was Mina. She was from Ireland, having answered a job advertisement that had not turned out to be quite what she had expected.

"The bastard," Sadie said as the Deputy recounted Mina's statement, although her voice was devoid of emotion. She was beginning to feel that no evil that humans could inflict on one another could surprise her anymore.

"So, we're looking at Silverman for facilitating prostitution, too," Cooper said, looking dazed. "This whole case escalated pretty damn fast."

"I've just called it in to Golightly," Sadie told them. "Depending on what Forensics find, and what information we get from the rest of his 'employees,' this is going to be a federal affair. It's wider than just Alaska."

Remembering how much the Coopers had originally resisted working with her, resentful of what they saw as Federal takeover, Sadie waited for a sarcastic comment from Jane or a grumble from the Sheriff, but the Coopers simply looked relieved.

"What about the murders?" Cooper asked.

"They'll stay with you – with us - for now, I imagine," Sadie said, "although they may get absorbed into the wider case."

There was a lot more that she wanted to say on that subject, but she decided to bite her lip until they had questioned Silverman. There were still too many loose threads that needed to be tied up, and questions that she needed answers to.

"Shall we wait for Forensics, or go and talk to him now? Your call," Sadie said to Cooper. He stood up by way of answer and they made their way to the Interrogation Room.

"We meet again," Sadie said to Erin Curtis, who was sitting with Silverman and looking furious. Perhaps she represented all of Silverman's 'friends.' It wouldn't be the first time that a lawyer was in the pay of organized crime.

"Good evening, Agent," Curtis said, pure venom in her voice. "You've kept my client waiting for some time."

"We're busy people," Sadie said, taking her seat and sweeping her gaze over the man opposite her. Unlike Higgins, Silverman sat upright in his chair and seemed to be trying to take up as much space as possible. Sadie could easily see how, in the wrong circumstances, Silverman could be a very intimidating guy. Carmen and Dana might well have been terrified of him. Add to that Higgins's allegation that Silverman had taken their passports, and it was easy to see how they had done whatever he had told them.

But did that excuse their actions? They could have confided in the families they worked for. Could have walked to the Station House at any time. Maybe it wasn't that easy – Silverman had threatened their families back home – or maybe, in a scenario that turned Sadie's stomach, they had been happy enough to go along with the pictures.

With the women dead, there were certain aspects of this whole mess that would never be known. The dead couldn't defend themselves.

"I have nothing to say," Silverman said before either Sadie or the Sheriff could ask him anything. "Whatever you think you've got on me, it's bullshit. And I will sue your asses for wrongful arrest."

The fear that Sadie had seen in Silverman in his office had gone, and she felt a shiver of foreboding, wondering where his newfound confidence had come from and what exactly Ms. Curtis had been advising her client.

“I think our asses are likely to be safe, Mr. Silverman,” Cooper said drily. “We have a lot of evidence against you. Anything you want to tell us?”

“I had nothing to do with those girls’ deaths,” Silverman said. “And I know nothing about any child pornography. I’m a legitimate businessman. Everyone in Anchorage knows me.”

Sadie wondered if that was supposed to be a threat. Silverman had press contacts, Cooper had told her that much, but they weren’t likely to be much use to him right now.

Once again, she spread out the pictures found in the Bait Shack, feeling the usual sweep of nausea as she avoided looking at them. This wasn’t something she could ever become immune to.

“Take that filth away from me,” Silverman snapped. Sadie saw that he was starting to sweat again – something that hadn’t happened when he had mentioned the murders.

“You don’t recognize it?” Sadie asked. “Because they were taken by women in your employ, and distributed by Joe Higgins and Michael DaCosta, on your behalf.”

Silverman’s right eye twitched, but he raised a smug eyebrow at her. “Do you have any proof of that, Agent?” he said. “Whatever the girls have been up to is nothing to do with me. As for Higgins and the other guy, I don’t know what you’re talking about. I’ve bought bait from the guys down at the commercial harbor, that’s all.”

Sadie glanced at Cooper, who was staring at Silverman, his jaw twitching in a way that she had come to recognize as barely contained anger.

“So why does your secretary have Higgins’s number as a contact in your office?”

Silverman shrugged. “Mina is my personal secretary. Sometimes she orders things for me when I don’t have time.”

Erin Curtis sighed impatiently. “Is this really all you have, Sheriff? You must know this isn’t enough to charge my client.”

“Maybe not,” Cooper snapped. “But Higgins’s statement is…and so is Mina’s. You can’t be a very good ‘boss,’ Silverman…she agreed to testify instantly. I think Immigration are going to want to have a nice chat with you too.”

Silverman’s eyes flickered towards his lawyer at the mention of Mina’s statement, and Sadie suppressed a smile. He hadn’t been expecting that.

“They’re trying to set me up,” he protested. “I don’t know anything about these pictures. It must have been happening without my knowledge…I’ve been distracted lately. Personal problems.”

He was lying, Sadie knew, and Silverman knew that they knew, but his defense might just work without anything concrete to tie him to the pictures. DaCosta, Carmen, and Dana were dead. There was no guarantee that the other au pairs would talk. Two statements would be enough to charge him, but Sadie doubted that it would hold up in court.

And witnesses could always disappear.

Silverman looked at Erin Curtis again and Sadie saw a look pass between them, as though Curtis was signaling her agreement to something. Silverman coughed and sat forward in his chair, an open expression on his face now.

“Look, I’ll be honest with you,” he said. “I’ve helped the girls out with work…some of them aren’t entirely legal, if you know what I mean. I’ll admit to that. It’s just, they’re so desperate, you know? Some of them come from such poor countries.”

“I’m sure your heart bleeds for them,” Sadie said, sarcasm dripping from every word.

“But apart from that,” Silverman continued, “I’ve done nothing wrong. They are trying to set me up. I would never involve myself in something so disgusting.”

Cooper glanced at Sadie.

“Shall we take a break until the morning, Agent Price?” he said quietly. “Let Mr. Silverman here have a good think about his options?”

Sadie nodded coolly, but even as she followed Cooper out of the room, she was fighting not to show her anxiety to the sleazy agent and his hard-faced lawyer.

“His argument could hold up if we don’t find anything more,” she said once they were down the other end of the corridor. She knew that Golightly would have his best agents taking this over, but Silverman’s obvious confidence had rattled her. “He’s going to attempt a plea deal on the lesser charges on immigration,” she said. It was a good strategy, she knew.

Cooper nodded, his lips pressed together so tightly they were a white line across his jaw.

“Of course, it’s probably just bravado,” Sadie countered, as much for her own sake as Cooper’s. “There are the other au pairs to interview, children still to talk and his computers and business accounts…”

She was interrupted by Cooper's phone ringing. As he strode back down to his office to answer it, Sadie made her way to the small reception. The Trooper who usually manned it was long gone. She leaned against the desk, thinking hard.

Silverman's whole demeanor when asked about the murders was entirely different than when he was questioned about his more obvious crimes. There also wasn't a shred of concrete evidence to link him to them.

And ultimately, it was the murders that she was supposed to be investigating.

"Everything okay?" She heard Cooper's voice and looked up to see him coming towards her, a big grin on his face as he passed her and reached for his coat.

"What's happened?" Sadie asked, ignoring his question.

"Forensics," the Sheriff said. "Silverman is too arrogant for his own good. They got into his 'hidden' files within minutes. It's all there, apparently: more pictures, links to websites…we've got him. This is all going to come crashing down around him."

Sadie smiled and gave a satisfied nod. Silverman would have to be an idiot not to confess now, if he ever wanted to be a free man again. Sadie had no doubt that his enterprise was any more than a tip of the iceberg, but at least for a while, some potential victims would be spared, and the children of Anchorage that were currently involved would be safe again. She thought of Mrs. Randolph and felt a wave of sadness.

Which brought the memory of Carmen's corpse hot on its heels. Sadie turned towards the window, feeling frustrated again.

"I suppose your guys will take over with Silverman now, at least for the trafficking ring," Cooper said. "At least we had the satisfaction of bringing him in."

Sadie didn't reply. She was looking out of the main Station House window onto the street. It was raining now, that kind of slushy rain that was still half snow, and it slid down the window in damp globules of dirty white. It would freeze over in the night, leaving the roads even more treacherous.

She wasn't looking forward to the drive back to the hotel and toyed with the idea of once again going to the saloon. It wasn't so much the whiskey that she wanted as a friendly face and a chance to forget about this case, just for a while, but she wondered what it said about her to be found in the saloon three nights in a row.

The daughter of a known local alcoholic. She had seen friends of her father's – or acquaintances, as he didn't really have friends anymore – in there before. Usually, Sadie couldn't give a damn what other people thought, but she had no wish to be tarred with the same label as a man she detested.

But neither did she want to go back to the motel while it was still evening, to spend the rest of the day alone with her thoughts.

"What is it, Price? You're still not happy with what we've done here today? This is all kudos for you; you've just handed Golightly a cut and dried pornography ring that could turn out to be nationwide, at the same time as finding our killer. You could get your name in the papers. So could we," he said, sounding more than a little proud. Sadie had no wish to take away the satisfaction of bringing down Silverman from him, but she also needed to voice her thoughts.

"I still don't think it's him. The murders. Or that he even had anything to do with them. Any evidence is purely circumstantial. It's going to get all thrown in together, and the murder charges probably won't even make it to court without any forensics. They'll just get dropped, and no one will care because the child trafficking ring will be stopped, and it will just be assumed Carmen and Dana were killed as part of it all."

Cooper looked bemused. "Isn't it just common sense at this stage? Silverman has the means, the motive, and the contacts. And the girls were trafficking the kids for him. Even if it turns out not to be him, it has to be someone inside the ring. Something more concrete will turn up when your guys start going over all this. Maybe even more bodies. There's still a lot of work to be done, Price. And like I said, we still have the receipts to go through until then."

"They were always a long shot," Sadie murmured. She was still looking out of the window, watching a battered snow plough go past at a crawling pace. A piece of green tinsel that had seen better days hung off the exhaust pipe.

"I know you're used to looking at these things through a different lens," Cooper began, sounding cautious. Sadie put up a hand, cutting him off mid-sentence.

"It isn't that I have some fixation for serial killers, Cooper, however that might come across. I'm trained to look at things from a behavioral perspective, and this just isn't right."

"People don't always behave how you expect them to," Cooper pointed out.

"There are always exceptions," Sadie countered, "But actually, most people are predictable, at least when we are talking about murder and serious crime. There is nothing about the way that Carmen and Dana were killed that fit with it being Silverman or even anything to do with him. Think about it: investigating their murders has blown his whole enterprise wide open. There is no way he would want any attention brought either to the harbor or to his au pair agency. Silverman is someone who cares very much about whether or not he goes to jail."

"And you think that whoever killed Carmen and Dana doesn't?" Cooper asked quietly. Sadie looked at him. He was regarding her seriously and she realized that he was taking everything that she was saying on board.

He believed her.

"No, I don't," she said. "Not as much as he cares about desecrating their bodies. Teaching them a lesson. I've been saying it from the start; it was *personal.* If it had been Silverman, it would have been about protecting his business interests."

"He could have wanted them to be an example to anyone else thinking of crossing him," Cooper suggested, but he sounded as though even he wasn't convinced by his own suggestion. He answered himself before Sadie could, echoing her thoughts. "But why take the risk of using the harbor?"

The Sheriff tapped his thigh, looking frustrated. "Okay, Price, let's say you're right. What evidence is there for any other scenario? We have nothing other than a pair of boots on a grainy video. And getting a warrant for the information attached to those receipts is likely to be on the back burner now."

"We check the records, nationwide, for any records of unsolved murders of au pairs, specifically. And maybe," Sadie hesitated, then gave voice to something that had been at the edge of her thoughts all day, "we go further back, and look at historical cases of abuse *by* au pairs. It's another long shot, because these things often go unreported, but it's a hunch I need to check out."

Cooper looked surprised, and she could tell, far from convinced.

"Think about it," Sadie said, "Why target au pairs, specifically? I know we've only got two victims, but just humor me a moment."

"I don't know...some kind of perverted fetish, maybe?" Cooper looked as though his words had left a bad taste in his mouth, his lips pursed like a man sucking limes.

"Maybe," Sadie conceded. "But there was no evidence the victims had been sexually assaulted. Of course, the crabs may have destroyed the evidence."

Now Cooper just looked as though he wanted to vomit. "The inside of your head is a dark place, Price," he winced.

"In our line of work, it has to be. Those bodies…the killer hated the victims, or something that they represented."

Cooper shook his head. "Who hates au pairs?"

"Someone who has been hurt by them."

They stared at each other, and Sadie could see that he was giving her words considerable thought. After a few moments he broke their gaze, rubbing a hand over his eyes.

"I can't process all this now," he said, and he sounded exhausted. "Let's go over it again in the morning."

Sadie almost wanted to apologize to him for ruining his evening. The day should have ended on a high, with the victory of getting a confession out of Higgins and bringing Silverman in. But she knew that she wouldn't sleep until she had shared her theory.

"There's nothing we can do now," she agreed. "We both need to sleep. I'll see you in the morning." She walked towards the door, pausing with her fingers around the handle to look back over her shoulder at him.

"There's one way that we will know if my theory is correct," she said quietly. Cooper frowned.

"What's that?"

"If another body turns up."

She stepped out into the cold.

CHAPTER TWENTY FOUR

He looked down at the woman and smiled to himself. She looked so fresh and innocent lying there, as though she was asleep.

In a natural sleep, that was, rather than the one that he had just administered to her by way of syringe. By the time she woke up, if she ever woke up, it would be too late.

He knelt down by her side and pushed her long hair away from her face almost tenderly. With her round face and long eyelashes, she looked almost like a child, but of course he knew better. She wasn't innocent; none of them were, and they deserved everything that was coming to them. He was doing the world a favor, really, even if no one was ever likely to thank him for it.

But that didn't matter. That wasn't the kind of recognition he wanted. No, what he wanted was for the world to know what these women were, underneath their sweet facades. What they were really about. He knew his role and had resigned himself a long time ago to the fact that it was unlikely he would ever get the accolades he deserved for what he was doing here. He was an avenging angel, but he knew that wider society would see him as some kind of devil.

But that was only because they were incapable of spotting the real devils in their midst. People could be so stupid, never questioning what was in front of them, never stopping to ask the right questions. And even when they did, there were always excuses made. The real evildoers never got what they deserved.

Now though, he would make sure that they did.

He picked up his knife, a surgical tool that he had sharpened to perfection, and slid it down the girl's cheek, allowing himself a frisson of pleasure. He always enjoyed this bit. Maybe next time, he would do this part while his victim was awake, although that might mean that the lines wouldn't be so precise. He wondered if there was any kind of drug that he could give them that would render them unable to move, but conscious enough to know what was happening to them.

The thought of it made him smile. He imagined the young woman beneath him, staring up at him helplessly, imagining the rush of seeing the terror in her eyes as he got to work on her. Picturing the terror grow as he lowered her into the hold, and she started to realize the fate that awaited her. It was tough to get the dosage and timings right, and he knew some of them might not wake up before the crabs had killed them bite by tiny bite. But with something like that, they would be aware of the whole thing. Aware but unable to help themselves.

It seemed to him that would be a more fitting punishment. He would have to look into it, do some more research. But for now, this would have to do.

And he needed to move quickly if he was going to get her into the hold without being noticed. This one wouldn't be found for a couple of days, by his reckoning. He had taken other steps to make sure that idiot Sheriff Cooper and his Fed girlfriend didn't discover his victim before she was dead.

He had seen them, poking around the harbor and checking all the boats, and he knew exactly what it was they were looking for. The rumors were going around like wildfire, and the place was on edge and crackling with paranoia. A lot of the fishermen and dockhands were illegal workers, and had other scams going on, and the recent police presence had everyone on edge.

He was taking a risk then, killing again so soon, but he hadn't been able to resist when she had gotten in touch. It was becoming a drug to him now, the only real pleasure that he had experienced for years. He couldn't let the Sheriff and his friends take that away from him.

And it was more important than that, too. These women needed to be obliterated, to be destroyed. Even if he received no pleasure from it, he knew he had to continue. The adrenaline rush was just the icing on the cake. He needed to keep reminding himself of what was really at stake; otherwise he ran the risk of getting sloppy, and that would never do.

He pried open his captive's mouth with gloved fingers and saw her tongue, pink and lolling to the side, relaxed from all the diazepam. It would be a nice prize, to go with his rapidly growing collection, a reminder of his mission. He felt like a Native warrior, taking a piece of his enemies to remind himself of his victory over them and to dishonor them even in death.

He was humming to himself as he started to cut.

CHAPTER TWENTY FIVE

By the time Sadie was halfway down her glass of whiskey, she had stopped feeling guilty about her new daily drinking habit. The whiskey calmed her mind, taking the edge from her frustration, which had her gritting her teeth on the drive over to the saloon.

She knew, in her gut, that Silverman wasn't the killer that they were looking for; and as much as Sheriff Cooper was right that nothing more could be done today, Sadie couldn't shake the sense of urgency that curled deep in the pit of her stomach, like a warning of things to come. Even the whiskey wasn't working on that.

Maybe a few more glasses, Sadie thought.

"I take it last night with the cute guy from the mall didn't go so well, huh?" Caz said sympathetically, as she finished serving a customer and came over to lean across the bar from Sadie. She wondered where Jenny and Emily were tonight. Upstairs, perhaps, watching holiday movies, Sadie thought wistfully as she remembered doing the same thing with Jessica while their father, too, had been at a bar, although not for the same reasons as Caz.

In fact, her father was likely at this bar, although it hadn't been owned by Caz then, who was from out of town.

She blinked in momentary confusion at Caz's words, having forgotten all about Toby.

"It was a work thing, really," she said flatly. "Best not to mix the two."

"In your line of work," Caz pointed out, "how else would you ever meet anyone? If you're going to keep turning the Sheriff down..."

Sadie couldn't help but smile at that. Caz was incorrigible.

"What was that about the Sheriff?" a voice asked behind her. Sadie swiveled round on her stool to see Deputy Jane Cooper hauling herself onto the stool next to her. She looked as bad as Sadie felt, with red-rimmed eyes that had heavy bags underneath them.

"Jane," Caz said warmly. "I don't see you in here too often. Not off-duty, anyway."

"It's been one of those days," Jane murmured. "One of those weeks, actually. A bottle of Bud please, Caz." She tucked her dark bob over one ear and smiled weakly at Sadie.

"Good work today. I'm so happy we've nailed Silverman." She seemed, Sadie noticed gratefully, to have forgotten the mention of her brother.

"Thanks, but you played a big part in that too, working with the kids' families," Sadie said. She wondered if Jane would feel resentful that the case had been passed to Sadie's fellow FBI agents now that it had escalated. When Sadie had first arrived and been assigned to a murder case with the Coopers, the Sheriff had been wary, but Jane had been outright rude in her hostility. Sadie still felt amazed at the sense of growing solidarity after such a difficult start.

Jane's next words reassured her.

"I'm glad my part in it is over to be quite honest with you," she said." It's the hardest thing that I've ever had to work on. Those poor kids," she shuddered. "It doesn't bear thinking about. I mean, I know you hear about this type of stuff all the time but to think that it's been happening here, in Anchorage, right under our noses…I can't quite get my head around the sheer evil of it, you know?"

Sadie nodded. "Yeah, I do know," she said softly, taking another swig of her whiskey and feeling even less guilty now that Jane was here to drown her sorrows alongside her.

Caz brought Jane's bottle of beer over, looking up at the clock as she did so. She looked worried.

"Is something wrong, Caz?" Sadie asked as she saw the bartender look up at the clock again as though checking her eyes were correct the first time.

"I'm sure it's nothing," Caz said with what seemed like forced cheerfulness. "I mean, the weather is awful so getting a cab might take longer than usual, but Jenny and Emily should be back by now."

"Oh?" Sadie asked, keeping her tone light even as a slither of dread started to make its way up her spine.

"Yeah," Caz continued. "Emily had a few hours off while Jenny went for dinner at a friend's house. She was supposed to pick her up and bring her back here. I was expecting them about an hour ago, but you know what kids are like. Maybe I'll give the mom a call."

The slither of dread intensified.

Next to her, Jane had put her bottle down and was looking shaken. As Caz moved away, she whispered to Sadie, "You don't think…"

"Let's wait and see if she turns up," Sadie said, pushing the rest of her whiskey away from her. She had a feeling that she might need to be sober.

The door to the saloon opened and Jenny came running in, her ponytail whipping around her head. Sadie breathed a sigh of relief, but then froze as she saw that Jenny's face was streaked with tears.

And that she was alone.

"Baby?" Caz said, moving quickly from behind the bar to gather Jenny to her. "What is it? Where's Emily?"

Jenny let out a sob.

"She didn't come to pick me up," she said, wiping her nose with the back of her hand. "So, Mary's mom drove me here in the car. We tried to call Emily again and again, but her cell is making a funny noise!" Her words ended on a wail, and she buried her face in Caz's shoulder.

"Oh my God," Jane whispered. Her face had gone white. Sadie tried not to panic, her head running through all of the likely and more benign scenarios to explain the au pair's disappearance.

"Oh, honey I'm sure she's fine," Caz said, although she looked worried. "Perhaps she lost her phone and got held up."

Jenny shook her head frantically. "No, Mom," she wailed, "you don't understand. She went to meet a man she met on the computer. She told me it was a secret."

As Caz looked confused, Sadie slid off her stool and walked towards mom and daughter, her heart pounding erratically against her ribcage.

"Caz," she said quietly, "let's go upstairs. There's something I need to tell you. I think Emily is in danger."

As Caz straightened up, frowning, Sadie motioned for Jane to come with them. There was no doubt in her mind that the killer had Emily.

And now they were running out of time to find her alive.

CHAPTER TWENTY SIX

Caz sent Jenny into the bathroom to wash her face while Sadie explained. Although she told her only the bare minimum of facts – even if she was authorized to, she wasn't going to let Caz know about just how the au pairs had been killed – the barkeeper was looking more and more as though she was going to faint by the second. She groped behind her for the bed, sitting down heavily.

Caz and Jenny lived in a small suite of rooms above the saloon, with faded décor and battered furniture. Pictures of Caz and her daughter were everywhere, some including Emily, and crayon drawings by Jenny seemed to be pinned to every available piece of wall. It was well-loved but cramped: a bedroom shared by them both, a lounge and kitchenette, bathroom, and a small room that doubled as both a study and a place for Emily to sleep. They were in there now, while Jane went through Emily's computer. Unlike Carmen, she had the sense to password-protect it.

"So, you're telling me local au pairs have been going missing," Caz echoed Sadie's words, "and turning up dead?" Sadie could hear the horror in her voice. Caz sounded on the verge of a panic attack, with only the need to take care of Jenny keeping her calm.

"Yes. But Emily may be safe and well; this is just a precaution," Sadie said, wishing that she believed that herself. They had already called the hospital and there was no indication that Emily had been in an accident. She had called Cooper and he was on his way, sounding as stricken on the phone as she felt. She knew that Cooper would have come to the same inevitable conclusion that she had; Emily had been taken by the harbor killer. The circumstances were just too familiar; like Carmen and Dana, she had been arranging to meet a man on the internet. Like them, she was a local au pair.

The difference, of course, was that there was nothing to indicate that Emily had been abusing Jenny – although Sadie knew that she would have to ask Jenny a few questions– and Emily hadn't been working for Silverman.

Which ruled out any lingering possibility that the killer was indeed working for Silverman. Sadie had been right; but right now, she had never wanted so badly to be wrong.

Jenny came into the room, looking very pale and very small.

"Is Emily going to be okay?" she asked, tears welling in her eyes. For a moment Sadie couldn't speak.

She didn't want to have to lie.

"I hope so, Jenny," she said at last, crouching down beside the little girl. "We're all going to do our very best to find her. But I'm going to have to ask you some questions about you and Emily and this man she was going to meet. I know she wanted you to keep it a secret, but if we're going to find her, we need to know absolutely everything that you do. That okay?"

Jenny nodded and wiped her eyes. She drew her shoulders back and lifted her chin up, a look of determination on her freckly little face that looked so much like her mother's.

"All I know," she said in her best grown-up voice, "Is that she was excited that she was going to meet a man from her computer. I don't think she was going to tell me, but I knew that she had a secret 'cos she was acting all funny when I asked her what she was going to do today. I kept asking and asking so she told me, and she asked me if her outfit was pretty. She said not to tell Mommy because she has a boyfriend back home and she thought Mommy would be mad at her. She went red. I think her boyfriend is mean to her anyway because she always cries when she has been on the phone to him."

Jenny stopped talking abruptly and clamped her mouth shut.

"That's really good, Jenny," Sadie reassured her. "You're really helping Emily by telling us this. Is there anything else you can think of? Did she tell you anything about the man or where she was going to meet him?"

Jenny shook her head. "No. Just that he sounded nice, and they were going for coffee."

"She didn't say where? Think hard, Jenny," Sadie urged.

"No. I would remember," Jenny said seriously.

"Thank you, sweetie." Sadie stood back up, feeling her knees twinge from where she had been crouching.

"You will find her, won't you?" Jenny pleaded, staring up at her. "I love Emily so much. She's like my big sister."

Caz looked as though she would burst into tears as she pulled her daughter to her, kissing her on the top of her head.

"Agent Price and the Deputy are doing everything they can, Emily," she said in a shaky voice that sounded nothing like the Caz that Sadie was familiar with. She locked eyes with Sadie, and she could see the terror in the saloon owner's eyes as she thought about the possibilities that awaited Emily.

"She could still turn up," Sadie said, but her voice sounded hollow, and she knew that she didn't believe that herself. She knew what had happened to Emily -she just didn't know who, or where. The things that they needed to know if they were to have any hope of saving her.

"I'm going to go and put Jenny to bed," Caz said. "Try and keep her in her routine." She led the girl out, nodding to Sadie and Jane, who was hunched over the computer, clicking away furiously with an intense expression on her face.

"I doubt if she's going to get any sleep unless we find Emily," Sadie said with a sigh, turning to Jane. "Anything?"

"Give me a minute; I think I'm going to be able to get into her social media accounts. If she has been messaging on the same app as Carmen, then I'll see it."

Sadie sat down on the edge of the bed, feeling useless and wishing the Sheriff would hurry up and arrive. She had already searched through Emily's meager belongings and found nothing.

"I'll go to the harbor," Sadie decided, standing up. "That's where he's going to take her at some point. The harbormaster will still be there, so we can get an idea of what boats will be docked tonight."

Jane looked at her over the rim of her glasses. "Don't you want to wait for Logan? Not that you can't do it by yourself," she said hurriedly, "But it could be dangerous. If we're going to search the boats it will take the three of us again, won't it?"

Sadie wanted to curse with impatience, but she knew that Jane was right. It would be dangerous – and entirely against protocol – to go into a potential murder scene alone and without back-up. After everything that had happened back in D.C., she should know that better than anyone. But just sitting around while poor Emily was potentially being drugged and left to be consumed by crabs was driving her crazy.

"I'll give him twenty minutes," she said eventually. "I know you're right, but what if he's already got her on a night fishing boat and it's out at sea? We can send out a recall, and check the logs, but by the time we get to her it might be too late."

"But what if she hasn't been taken?" Jane said reasonably. "We can't order a harbor search without more evidence, surely?"

"I can," Sadie said. "If it turns out to be unfounded, I'll take the heat from Golightly."

Jane was about to say something when she clicked on the wireless mouse and gave a mirthless smile. "You might not need to. I'm in."

Sadie went to stand behind her, watching as Jane scrolled through Emily's messages.

"It looks as though she was on a few dating sites," Jane said. "She really must have been unhappy with her boyfriend. I wonder what it was about this guy that made her take the plunge to meet up?"

"Sociopaths can be surprisingly charming," Sadie muttered darkly.

Her stomach sank as the same app that Carmen had been using flashed up. Sure enough, the same username they had spotted on Carmen's laptop was there, and there were a ton of messages between him and Emily. Jane clicked on the few most recent.

"It's him. They arranged to meet today. But look," Jane pointed at the timer, "He was talking to her at the same time that he was talking to Carmen. He arranged them both together."

"He's planning them in advance, not just one by one." Sadie shook her head. "It's like some kind of crusade. Can you bring this back to the Station? We need to get Forensics on this, to see if they can track his username and find out who else he has been messaging. Then we can tie him to Dana – and potentially others."

Jane nodded and shut the computer down. They called goodbye to Caz, assuring her they would be in touch as soon as they knew anything, and then carried the computer down and out of the saloon.

Sheriff Cooper was outside, jumping out of his snowcat. His gaze went straight to Sadie.

"I should have listened to you," he said.

"You did listen," Sadie said. "There was no way of preventing this; he's moving fast now, and there's hardly any gap between victims. He doesn't care about getting caught, he just wants to kill as many women as possible before he does."

Jane looked nauseated as she climbed into the snowcat. "I'll take the truck," Sadie said to the Sheriff.

As she pulled out, her stomach was churning and her hands shaking on the steering wheel. They had to find Emily, for Caz and Jenny's sake. The little girl's face haunted her on the drive to the harbor, her words nagging at Sadie's conscience, reminding her of another loss and another young woman.

One that hadn't been found in time.

You will find her, won't you? She's like my big sister.

CHAPTER TWENTY SEVEN

The harbor again. Sadie was starting to get sick of the place. Its now familiar smells assailed her senses as they made their way to the harbormaster's office. Thankfully, there was a light still on in the small cabin.

Jane lingered behind, taking a cursory look around the harbor and questioning any remaining dockhands, while Sheriff Cooper went with Sadie to speak to Robert Holmes. She could feel the need for urgency radiating from the Sheriff's body and knew that the same was coming from her.

They had to find Emily. She couldn't bear the thought of breaking it to Jenny that she was never going to see her friend again. Unlike the other victims, it seemed clear that there was nothing untoward in Emily's treatment of the young girl in her care, which raised the question of why Emily had been targeted.

Sadie suspected it was random. This wasn't about who Emily was or anything she had done; this was a killer responding to his own warped view of the world. Cooper thought it was more simple than that; that the killer had known about the abuse but had made a mistake with Emily. Either way, they were no closer to finding the missing au pair. The 'why' didn't matter right now; they just needed to know the 'who' and more importantly, the 'where.'

It was the last detail that they were hoping the harbormaster, Robert Holmes, could help with.

When Holmes answered the door to his cabin office, his face lit up when he saw Sadie, a knowing glint in his eyes that made her immediately uncomfortable.

"Back again, Agent Price? You don't seem to be able to keep away," he smiled, amused at his own joke.

"We're here about a missing woman," Cooper snapped behind her before she could answer. Holmes's eyes went to the Sheriff, noticing him for the first time and looking disappointed.

"Can we come in?" Sadie said. "It would be better if we weren't overheard." They didn't want to alert anyone to their presence before it was necessary, either. She wouldn't put it past some of the captains to get their boats out as quickly as possible rather than have their night fishing disrupted by yet another search.

"If you must," the harbormaster said with a long-suffering smile, opening the door to let them in. He switched off a small radio in the corner and motioned them to a couch underneath the window. It was threadbare and had seen better days, but the harbormaster's technical equipment was state of the art. Sadie wondered how much it paid, looking after the docks.

"So, how can I help?" he asked, taking a seat behind his desk and crossing his long legs in front of him. He looked lean and fit, Sadie thought, and probably stronger than his size.

Strong enough to drag bodies into holds?

"You know about the bodies found here," the Sheriff said.

"Of course. Though as requested, I have said very little to the men. All these searches are causing quite a stir among the men, as you can imagine. I appreciate the urgency of this, but..."

"I'm not sure you do," Sadie interrupted him. Her eyes flashed with anger. "We are talking about serial murders, Mr. Holmes, taking place on your watch. We now have another young woman missing, and we have reason to believe she has been taken by the same person – and is therefore likely to turn up in the same manner. It is imperative that we find her, and quickly."

Holmes sat back in his chair, the smile gone from his face.

"Agent, I don't appreciate the insinuation that I am somehow responsible for this."

Sadie sighed impatiently. They didn't have time for this man's ego. She was grateful when the Sheriff took over, sounding as impatient as she felt.

"We need your logs, Mr. Holmes," he said, and there was demand rather than request in his tone. "As well as searching the boats currently docked, we need to know which boats are about to go out, and which ones went out at which time. We're working within a certain timeframe here, so if we can tie that to a particular ship, we can locate the potential victim a lot quicker than just by an arbitrary search."

Holmes shifted in his seat, and Sadie thought that he looked obviously uncomfortable with the request.

"That's official information you're asking for there, Sheriff. Don't you need some kind of warrant for that?"

"Mr. Holmes," Sadie interrupted, resisting the temptation to scream at the less than cooperative harbormaster. "We are trying to prevent a murder. And you are holding us up. This is starting to look a little like deliberate obstruction. Is there something you want to tell us?"

The harbormaster made a show of looking affronted. "Are you implying that I have something to hide, Agent Price?"

Sadie swallowed her anger and spoke very deliberately, enunciating each word. "Mr. Holmes. Please. We need to see those logs."

The harbormaster sighed dramatically. "Very well," he said. He got up and moved over to a filing cabinet in the corner of the office. Almost deliberately taking his time, Sadie thought.

"Are the files not on the computer?" Cooper asked. "It's a nice piece of equipment you have there."

The harbormaster had the grace to look embarrassed as he brought a logbook over to them. "I haven't had time to transfer everything over yet. The digital system is fairly new and as you can imagine, our wireless isn't exactly reliable. Pen and paperwork for me, Sheriff."

"Can't argue with you there," Cooper said, opening the logbook. Sadie leaned over to read it with him, her pulse pounding with anticipation. Finally, they might start to get somewhere. They knew that Emily had met the killer in the afternoon, which meant that she had been with him a maximum of seven hours. If she was already on a boat, it had to be one that had come in since that time but wouldn't be unloaded until the morning, or one that had not long gone out. That should give them a narrowed down list of potential locations – and suspects.

It should have been straightforward, if it wasn't for the fact that half of the records were missing. Sadie stared at the information in front of her, trying to make head and tail of it.

"This ship here, the *Sleepless Sally*," she asked, pointing at an entry in the log. "What time did it go out? Or is she still docked?"

"She's gone out," Holmes said, then offered no further information.

"At what time?" Sadie asked, impatiently. Holmes frowned, his brow creasing.

"I'm not entirely sure," he admitted, flushing slightly when the Sheriff groaned with impatience. "Sometime early this afternoon, I believe."

That was close. "The boats that went out between then and now," Sadie said, "can they be recalled?"

The harbormaster looked at her incredulously. "In the middle of a trawl?"

"For God's sake, man!" the Sheriff finally erupted, getting to his feet. "We are trying to prevent a murder!"

Holmes blinked rapidly, looking nervous. "Sheriff," he said apologetically, "this is hardly typical. No one usually needs the logs but me. And I have no jurisdiction over the captains. I appreciate your urgency, but I can't force them to turn their boats around. They have quotas to fill, and often don't get paid if they're short. I can radio out to them, but the chances of them coming in until the morning are slim."

"Do that," Sadie said, getting up and tucking the logbook under her arm. "We can try, at least. Otherwise, we will be back tomorrow to search those boats – but by then, our missing victim will be dead. In the meantime, Mr. Holmes, if we can just borrow this to make a list of currently docked boats that we need to search?"

Holmes nodded and waved a hand at her. "Sure, Agent Price, go ahead." Sadie thanked him with a polite smile that she knew didn't quite reach her eyes. It wasn't lost on her how little concern the harbormaster seemed to have for a missing and potentially murdered young woman.

They stepped outside, and Cooper took a few deep breaths of the cold air. "I nearly lost it in there," he admitted. "What is wrong with these people?"

Sadie shook her head. "I hear you. But let's get this list of boats divvied up. If we take them one by one, it will be a lot quicker, and we might just get done before everyone goes home."

"No one is going home until we're done," Cooper said, his jaw jutting. Sadie nodded and then started to scan the logbook again, her mind working rapidly.

Thanks to Holmes' inept record keeping, there were going to be a lot of boats to search.

CHAPTER TWENTY EIGHT

It was going to be a long night.

Sheriff Logan Cooper made his way towards the first boat on his list, doing a quick scan of the information that the harbormaster had provided. Or rather, lack of information. He wondered if Agent Price had picked up on just how reluctant the guy seemed to be to help and knew that she would have. Price was as sharp as a tack, and as much as Cooper had initially wanted to write her off as another Fed who would prove to be up their own ass, she was a damn good detective.

He had so wanted to dislike her when she had first turned up. His previous, admittedly, fairly limited experience with FBI agents was that they saw Troopers like him as no more than hicks. Once they were on a case he was expected to step back, regardless of how much good policing he and his team had done up to then. It was a territorial thing. This was *his* turf.

He had grown up with his father's stories about the Feds, too. Like him, his dad had made it from state trooper to Sheriff by the age of thirty, back down in Juneau, and he too had gotten pissed at federal agents muscling in on his bigger cases. Upsetting the locals and throwing their weight around.

But Price – Sadie – was different. For all her fancy BAU training, she never attempted to talk down to him and she relied on her gut as much as her academic smarts, which was something that Cooper appreciated.

It didn't even bother him that she was right most of the time, either.

Not that they didn't clash, and often. From that first day, when they had both been on edge, expecting the other to be hostile, to that very morning when she had bitten his head off, there was often a tension between them, but it had settled into what he thought of as mostly healthy banter between colleagues. Even she and Jane were starting to get friendly, and that had gotten off to a very shaky start. The thought of being the mediator between his often-hotheaded sister and Sadie Price was nowhere near the top of Cooper's to-do list.

In short, they had a good working relationship. If there was anything that was likely to disrupt that, it was the way Cooper felt his whole body go tight when he saw men like the sales manager at the mall and even the harbormaster look Price up and down like a piece of meat, all laid out ready for their consumption. It made him want to punch someone. Hard.

Cooper was an old-fashioned guy, brought up by a traditional man who believed in treating women with respect, opening doors and not cussing in front of them. Their father had been horrified when Jane, his only daughter, had decided to be a State Trooper as well as her older brother, although he was secretly proud of her now. But as much as Cooper was trying to tell himself that his upbringing was the reason that he was so protective of Price, he had the uncomfortable feeling that it went a little deeper than that. Sadie was attractive, in a windswept, not at all trying kinda way, and in spite of her evident toughness there was a subtle vulnerability to her that appealed to the alpha male in him.

Of course, she would probably break his nose if she knew he was even thinking that way.

He watched her moving down the harbor with that purposeful way she had, completely focused on the task at hand, before he turned away and boarded the boat, momentarily putting Sadie Price out of his mind.

He was as invested as she was in finding the killer, more than that, in intercepting his latest kill. He didn't want to see any more young women lying on Pete's slab in the same state as the first two victims, and now that they knew that the current girl was Caz's au pair, the case had taken on yet another all too personal twist. Cooper liked Caz. She was a wealth of useful information and a staple figure in the local community. He didn't want to see her, or her little girl, upset.

The captain of the current boat eyed him with a look that Cooper was getting used to from the fishermen and workers at this harbor. They saw these searches as a nuisance, and even if they fully knew the purpose of them, Cooper doubted it would make any difference. These were hard bitten men with livings to make and often families to feed, and that took precedence over everything else.

"Another search, Sheriff?" the man said with a weary sigh as Cooper flashed his badge.

"I'm afraid so," he said, his tone short. "I'd like to start with the hold."

The captain raised an eyebrow. "There's nothing down there. On account of the fact that we haven't been able to take her out yet, because your search is holding us up."

Cooper ignored his barb and motioned towards the entrance to the hold. Rolling his eyes, the captain gave the nod for one of the fishermen to open it up, and then he led the way down the ladder, as though he didn't trust the Sheriff to go down there by himself.

Ten minutes later, after a quick look around the empty hold and the rest of the boat, including lockers, Cooper jogged down the harbor towards the next boat. His radio crackled with updates from Jane and Agent Price.

Nothing. Cooper looked up at the moon that was riding the clouds and wondered what the chances were of them finding Emily before the sedatives and the crabs had done their gory work.

Probably slim to none, he admitted to himself. The killer had to know by now that this would be the first place that they would look, and that Emily would be noticed as missing. Or perhaps Emily hadn't mentioned what time she needed to get back? He shook his head at the risk these women took meeting strangers online, and without giving anyone details of where they would be and when they would be back. It was basic safety measures 101.

But then, whoever expected to fall into the clutches of a violent killer? In a just world, no one should have to prepare for those circumstances, let alone young women who should have their whole lives ahead of them.

Ten boat searches later and Cooper was getting restless as the chances of finding Emily alive seemed to slip farther and farther away. He boarded the next one on his list, noting immediately that one of the fishermen, a redhead with a thick neck and bulging eyes, looked wary as he approached, his eyelid flickering in a way that made Cooper wonder what the man had to hide. As he addressed the captain, it was the redhead that he kept his eyes on.

"Can I take your name please, Sir?" he asked him. The redhead visibly flinched.

"Hank," he muttered. Cooper waited for the rest.

"Hank Smith," the captain replied, more helpfully. "Hank, show the sheriff down into the hold, please."

Hank glowered, as though he would rather toss Cooper overboard and leave him to the fishes, but he showed him down. Once again, nothing.

It was at the lockers that Hank grew even more tense. It came off him in waves as the captain opened his locker and motioned for Cooper to look inside. As unlikely as it was, Cooper half expected to find the missing tongues of the victims and had to stop himself from groaning with disappointment when the unmistakable smell of fresh cannabis hit him. He pulled the bag out and tossed it to the captain, who caught it out of reflex and then looked down, stunned, at what he was holding before turning to glare at Hank, who was stepping backwards across the deck.

"Think of this as your lucky night, Hank," Cooper said drily. "I'm not here on a drugs raid. Looks as though you have some explaining to do to your captain here, though."

He left them to sort it out among themselves and made his way off that boat and on to the next, moving even faster now as the sense of urgency grew. He radioed the others to let them know his position and give them an update.

Neither Price nor Jane had found any sign of Emily or anything untoward relating to her. Some hardcore pornography, a few bottles of fentanyl and some more cannabis, but no sign of the au pair or anything that could lead them to the killer. The frustration was evident in all of their voices.

They reconvened at the end of the harbor, and Cooper noticed the pinched look on Price's face and the wide-eyed apprehension on his sister's and felt an impotent rage at his own helplessness to do anything about it. He was the Sheriff, this was *his* town, and yet this killer was so far running rings around them all.

"It's possible," Price said, pushing tendrils of hair that had escaped from her braid back from her face, "that he's got wind of the search here and backed off." The tip of her nose and her cheeks were red from the cold where her scarf had worked its way loose around her neck, but she didn't seem to have noticed. Her eyes scanned the boats, ever watchful.

"In that case," Cooper replied, the frustration bubbling over into his voice, "we have no goddamn idea where else he could have taken her. If he decides to change his killing ground and method, we're back where we started: knowing nothing."

Jane visibly shuddered, looking up at her brother. A light from one of the nearby boats shone on her face and Cooper saw how tired his younger sister looked; it had been a heavy week for them all, and it was taking its toll on them.

"We could speak to the harbormaster again?" she suggested. "There's something slimy about him."

"I thought so too," Price agreed, and Cooper felt a twinge of satisfaction that he swiftly quelled. It was no business of his what the agent thought of the admittedly handsome harbormaster. "But I'm not sure there is anything more that he can – or will – tell us. The problem with this place, as we've found, is everyone seems to have something to hide, so no one is exactly cooperative."

"Then what are we supposed to do?" Cooper asked, rocking on his heels with impatience. "We might be able to use the receipts, computer data, and Forensics to track the killer, or he might turn up at the internet café again and we can get a better description…but all that will be too late for Emily."

"He'll be on to his next victim by then," Price said. "He's escalating, not leaving any time between victims. He probably has his next one already lined up on the dating sites. We need to issue this to the press now and warn women – au pairs, specifically – not to go on any internet dates."

"I'll get on that first thing in the morning," Jane said softly, "But what now? The boats that are out at sea, should we wait for them to come back? I know the time frames are close but…," she shrugged, echoing what all three of them felt; what else was there to do?

Price was scanning the harbor again, her brow creased in a way that Cooper now knew meant that she was thinking hard. Suddenly, she sprang into action and started jogging towards her vehicle. Motioning for them to follow her.

"Price, where are you going?" Cooper yelled impatiently, catching up with her. She swung around to face him, her eyes shining feverishly.

"Whoever the killer is, he's got access to the harbor, right?"

"Yes," Cooper said slowly, "we know that. So why are we leaving?"

"Because," she said, shaking her head as if at their own stupidity, "this isn't the only harbor, is it?"

"There's the private harbor," Jane said behind them. "But how would he have access to boats there and on the commercial ships? The working fishermen aren't generally making enough money to own a private boat of their own, even the captains."

"No, but dockhands could work both harbors, couldn't they?" Price argued even as she started to get into her truck. "And who really notices them? They are on and off the boats, here one day, gone the next. We've been too busy focusing on familiar faces around here, but this is a guy who works in the shadows."

"You're right," Cooper said, throwing open the door to the snowcat and motioning for Jane to get in. "Go. We're right behind you."

They pulled off, driving as fast as they could towards the private harbor at the edge of town. It was nearly midnight now, and time was slipping away fast.

"Do you think we'll find her?" Jane asked next to him. Cooper shook his head.

"I hope so."

They both knew that hope was all they had.

CHAPTER TWENTY NINE

As Sadie was expecting, the private harbor was silent. Cleaner and somehow fresher smelling than its commercial counterpart, the boats were newer and shinier than their well-used sisters. Some of them looked as though they had been docked for weeks, covered in tarp, and left until the weather and waves were less treacherous.

There were less boats to search here, but there was also less indication of which ones needed to be searched. The tiny harbormaster's cabin was empty and locked, and the whole place seemed to be deserted.

That also meant that there were no logs to find out which boat was likely to be the one they were looking for, or any indication of who had been on board what. While the private harbor was less likely to be a hotbed of criminal activity and needed less oversight, that also made it a good place for the killer to hide. They had overlooked it until now, and Sadie wanted to kick herself for her mistake.

"Oh, God," Jane said, looking around with wide eyes. "Where are we going to start?"

"We'll have to split up again," Sadie said. "And search everywhere. Take the boats that seem recently used first, of course. We'll take a third of the harbor each."

Jane nodded, bouncing on her heels and ready to get going, but Sheriff Cooper frowned as he looked around over the private harbor. An air of peacefulness lay over the place that was eerily at odds with the reason they were there.

"I don't think we should split up," he said. "We ought to stay together. This place is deserted; if the killer is still around, he could get the jump on us. Or at least, you two team up."

Sadie raised a furious eyebrow at him. This was no time for the Sheriff to turn all traditional on them. "Is that because we're women, Sheriff? I didn't spend my whole time at Quantico behind a desk, you know."

Jane crossed her arms and spoke before Cooper could answer. "I'm with Sadie. We're all armed, and we're running out of time, Logan. We need to find Emily."

The Sheriff sighed and nodded, but he didn't look happy about it. Ordinarily, Sadie might better appreciate his attempt to look out for them, but they didn't have time for his benign sexism right now.

She could look after herself, and so could Deputy Cooper, whereas Emily didn't have a chance against this guy, whoever he might turn out to be.

"All right, Price," Cooper said, although the reluctance was evident in his voice. "But we need to keep in constant communication with our locations. Stay on your guards. If our guy is using this place too, then he knows his way around here better than we do."

"Noted, Sheriff. I'll take the farthest end, and you start by the entrance maybe? Jane can take the middle boats. We can get through here in an hour."

The Coopers nodded, and Logan jogged back down towards the entrance to the harbor. As Sadie turned to go, Jane laid a hand on her arm. The Deputy wasn't a woman given to sentimentality, and Sadie blinked in surprise at her next words.

"Be careful, Price," the other woman cautioned. "After what happened on the last case..." Jane swallowed, unable to finish her sentence, and Sadie realized that it was the first time Jane had ever mentioned the culminating events of their last case out loud, where both Sadie and Jane had briefly been at the mercy of an unbelievably vicious killer. It had been traumatic, yet in the stoic nature of homicide cops, they had never discussed it with one another.

"I know," Sadie said softly. "It will be okay. We'll get this bastard...and find Emily." It was said with a lot more confidence than she felt. Jane lifted her chin, gave a determined nod and removed her arm before moving towards the nearest boat. Sadie jogged towards the far end of the harbor, ready to start the search.

She hoped that her last words to Jane would prove to be right, but she also knew that at this point, she was hoping that it wasn't a dead woman that they were looking for.

*

Sadie paused as she stepped off the last boat she had searched and looked around, listening to the sounds of the harbor. She thought that she had heard something, right on the periphery of her hearing, but she couldn't be sure. Moving as carefully and as quietly as she could, she made her way towards the next boat that she needed to search. She was nearly at the last of her quota and was beginning to think that she had been wrong, and the killer had never been anywhere near the smaller harbor. So far, nothing had been out of place.

She paused before boarding the next boat, listening carefully for the sound she was sure that she had heard. It was new, white, and glistening in the slip, and it looked recently used. She could see water gleaming on the deck and knew it had been out on the ocean very recently. Sadie felt her heart starting to beat a tattoo in her chest as her instincts caused goosebumps to raise on her skin. Whatever the sound was, it had come from this boat. The *Lovely Lass.*

She was about to radio her location to the Coopers when she saw a shadow move out of the corner of her eye.

On the deck of the boat.

Sadie froze, her mind running through a list of scenarios. Should she radio the Coopers to continue this search with her; but what if she was wrong and they missed something on their own searches? Or worse, she only alerted the killer to their presence, and he hurt Emily further before they could get to him?

With her heart in her mouth, Sadie dimmed the bulb on her flashlight and crept towards the *Lovely Lass*, using the harbor shadows as a cover. As she got closer, she wondered if she had been wrong. The deck looked empty, and she could hear nothing except the water caressing the side of the boat.

Still, a sixth sense told her that something was wrong.

Staying as low and quiet as possible, she boarded the *Lovely Lass*, creeping across the deck and using her dimmest bulb. Even with that, anyone aboard was likely to notice her now and her senses were on high alert as she moved forward, her spare hand close to her holster, ready to draw if she needed to.

She froze as she heard another noise. A rustling, that could have been a human or an animal – crabs in the hold? - or simply the wind. Holding her breath, she made her way towards the direction of the sound.

And then she realized where it could be coming from.

The hold.

CHAPTER THIRTY

It was so dark in the hold that the beam of Sadie's flashlight only seemed to highlight the depth of the shadows. She made her way carefully down the ladder, holding her breath against the intense smell of fish, crab, and mulch from the seabed.

The smell wasn't anywhere near as bad as the sound, though. The frenzied scuttling told her that the hold was full of crabs, who were very much alive and sooner or later would be hungry. She tried to blank the image of Carmen and Dana's bodies from her mind even as she prayed that she wasn't about to find Emily in the same state. That they would find her in time, or even that she was entirely wrong, and that Emily would turn up, safe as could be and wondering what the whole rescue operation was all about.

But Sadie was a realist, and as she stopped on the last rung of the ladder and swung her flashlight around the hold, it wasn't just crabs that she was looking for.

There were hundreds of them, a few of them with bodies as big as her torso, their legs as long as her arms with vicious looking pincers on the end of them. In the dark, they looked like huge spiders, reminding Sadie of a horror movie that she had seen once, and she forced herself to breathe deeply and slowly, trying not to panic.

She squinted through the hold, her eyes adjusting to the light, looking for any sign of Emily, swinging her flashlight slowly from side to side. The crabs tried to scuttle away from the light, intensifying the noise.

Then she saw it in the sweep of her light, a glimpse of soft brown flesh in contrast to the hard shells of the crabs. Taking a deep breath, Sadie plunged into the mass of crabs, kicking them away as she reached for what she could now see was a naked thigh. She pushed the crabs away from Emily, lifting the young woman up and out of them as best as she could. She let out a loud exhale of relief to feel that Emily's skin was warm, and then saw the girl's eyelids flicker. Not only was she alive but she hadn't been unconscious for long. As she hoisted her over one shoulder, nearly falling among the crabs as she tried to manage both Emily and her flashlight, Sadie saw that the girl had only a few bites from the crabs as yet. She had found her in time to save her.

Not that Emily was entirely unharmed, judging by the dried blood around her mouth. Her tongue, Sadie realized with a lurch of nausea. Still, at least she was alive.

Only as she reached the ladder did it occur to her that if Emily had not been in the hold very long, then the killer was likely to still be very near.

As she had the thought a shadow loomed over her, blocking what little moonlight came through the entrance to the hold. Sadie fumbled for her gun only to drop her flashlight into the hold below.

The blow hit her on the side of the head, causing her to drop Emily and lose her footing on the ladder. There was a flash of light, and she heard someone scream and then realized that it was her.

Then everything went dark.

*

Sadie blinked, but at first, she could make out only shadows. Her head was thumping with pain from where she had been hit, and as the memory of being attacked came back to her in a rush she tried to sit up, immediately reaching for her gun, only to simultaneously realize that her holster was empty and that her arms and legs were tied.

Then she realized that she was naked, and in the hold. Close to her – terrifyingly close – she heard the unmistakable scuttle of the crabs, and as she opened her mouth to scream a large hand was thrust over her mouth.

"Shut up," came a voice above her. A man loomed over her, holding her down. He had a head lamp on, and Sadie knew that it was only his presence and the light that were keeping the crabs from crawling all over her.

Emily, she thought in horror. *Where is Emily*? Her eyes darted from side to side, and she caught a glimpse of the other woman's long, dark hair next to her. Sadie wondered if she was still alive.

Then she looked up, into the face of the man who was holding them both captive.

The face of a killer.

She recognized him, although not at first. It wasn't a face that she knew, merely one that she had seen around the harbor, but as she caught sight of the crescent shaped scar above his eyebrow, she remembered the night that she had spoken to him. The dockhand whose friend had attempted to flirt with her.

He had been under their noses the entire time.

He saw the flicker of recognition in her eyes and smiled at her in a way that was almost friendly.

"I'm going to let go of your mouth," he said, "as long as you don't scream. No one will hear you – I've shut the hold." He jerked his head up to the entrance above his head. He was sitting on the bottom rung of the ladder, quite casually, as though they were just having a chat.

She could use that, she realized. Keep him talking. She nodded, and he slowly removed his hand. A crab moved just inches away from her head and she held her breath, telling herself not to scream.

"Can I sit up?" she asked. He laughed.

"So you can attempt to get free? I don't think so, Agent. You'll be fine where you are."

He was around thirty, with sharp features that could have been handsome were it not for the thinness of his lips and a mean look to his eyes. There was nothing, other than that scar, to distinguish him from the other dockhands milling around the harbors. Mr. Nobody.

Sadie glanced at his feet, which rested just above her on the ladder, and felt a hysterical giggle rising in her throat. There they were, the boots that marked him out as Terminal Seven Guy.

"Were you – are you – working for Silverman?" she asked, although she knew the answer even before his mouth curled in disgust.

"That thug? No, I'm not. Mike was though, the guy you chased into the shack on the islands. I hoped, when that happened, that you would think it was him, but no, you had to go on poking around, didn't you? Poking your nose in."

"I'm a federal agent," Sadie said reasonably. "It's my job. Still, you managed to evade us, didn't you? Until now," she added.

His eyes flashed with anger. "Until now? You think you're getting out of here?" His tone was arrogant now, his eyes mocking as he stared down at her, and Sadie was fighting not to give in to her fear. Not to let him see her terror.

It was hard, to be this vulnerable, naked and bound by the man that she had been hunting, and maintain an ounce of calm, but she knew that was her only chance of getting out of this alive. If she could keep the dockhand talking until the Coopers realized that she had disappeared and started to check the rest of the boats, then she might be able to save Emily.

"What's this all about?" she asked, sounding genuinely interested. Flattering him with her attention.

He took the bait, smiling mirthlessly as he answered her.

"You haven't figured any of it out? You're still hung up on Silverman, aren't you? Oh, I know all about his dealings; Mike DaCosta tried to get me on board. As though I would be interested in *that* filth." He spat into the mass of crabs. "Who hurts kids like that?" he said, his eyes wide with genuine outrage, seemingly unable to grasp the irony.

"It's disgusting, I agree," Sadie said, nodding and then wincing as the movement caused the wound on her head to throb even more. "So, you found out about Silverman's au pairs taking the pictures of the kids and decided to kill them?"

He shrugged, as though in agreement, but she saw something in his eyes that confused her. Surprise?

"But Emily doesn't work for Silverman," Sadie pressed, her mouth dry. "She hasn't done anything wrong. I know the little girl that Emily looks after, and she loves her. You could let her go," she suggested.

The dockhand laughed bitterly and leaned down, pressing his face close to hers, a look of pure rage in his eyes.

"You stupid bitch," he said coldly. "You've got this all wrong, haven't you? But thank you for confirming what I already knew. Those bitches deserved to die. And so does this one. They all do." He sat back up, glaring at her, and Sadie felt her heart thumping so hard she felt it would burst through her chest.

"You didn't know," she whispered, almost to herself, so that he had to lean forward again to hear her. She was beginning to feel tired, and her words seemed to be coming out more slowly than she wanted them to. She wondered how much damage his blow to her head had caused. "You didn't know Carmen and Dana were abusing the kids in their care. I was right; it's about them being au pairs."

"Well done, Agent. You deserve a medal," he said contemptuously.

She looked into his eyes and saw the void behind his anger.

"What did your au pair do to you?" Sadie asked him softly. He looked haunted at her question, his eyes glazing over as he stared into the past rather than the present. As he started to talk, Sadie carefully moved her wrists against the fishing rope that he had bound her with. If she had enough time, she might be able to work a hand free.

"After Mom died," he was saying in an almost sing-song voice, "My pop was never around. He was a fisherman, a good one, but the hours are long. He got me this au pair: a Ukrainian girl. Anna." He spat the name in disgust. "He thought she was amazing. So much so he married her. Wouldn't believe anything I said about her."

"She hurt you," Sadie said, trying to sound sympathetic. The truth was, she did have sympathy for the helpless young boy that he had been. Perhaps, if anyone had helped him, he wouldn't have become the monster that he was today.

But that wouldn't stop her taking him down if she could just get free.

Next to her, Emily felt cold.

"Yeah," he said, and she could hear the pain and rage in his voice. "She used to…do things to me. Then wash me in scalding water. When I cried…she threatened to tell my pop to lock me in his crab hold. Told me how they would kill me, bite by bite. I had nightmares every night for months. Started wetting the bed." A look of intense shame crossed his face.

"I'm sorry," Sadie said, meaning it. "She was evil. But not everyone is like that. Not everyone who looks after kids does that." Her words were coming out slowly, sounding thick in her mouth.

"No? But you just told me about Silverman's au pairs," he chuckled, but it was a dark sound that sent a shiver through Sadie. "So, I was right to kill them. And you, Agent, are on the wrong side."

"No," Sadie said, forcing suddenly heavy eyelids to stay open. She was drugged, she realized finally. Just as the others had been. Which meant the same fate awaited her. She would be left here with Emily, and the best that she could hope for was that she didn't come back around while the crabs made a meal of her. "You're wrong. Emily isn't like that. Emily is good, and you don't need to kill her."

He stood up and looked down at her, pity in his eyes. "You really believe that, don't you?" he said, shaking his head. "You don't see that I'm doing the world a favor, getting rid of these bitches. That includes this one here. Even if she hasn't started her evil tricks yet, it's only a matter of time. They're all the same. It's a shame you came down here, Agent. I would rather not have killed you. But you've left me with no choice."

Sadie forced herself to turn her head, looking around to make out what she could of the hold. There had to be a way out, something that she could do to help herself…She struggled against the stupor that was creeping over her whole body now and threatening to drag her under. She had to fight it, she told herself, had to keep herself awake.

Just a few feet away, there was a life-ring on the wall with a cord. A cord that, if pulled, would emit a siren loud enough to be heard across the harbor. If she could just get to it…there was room to pull her hand from the rope now, but she was all out of energy to move.

"You…have a choice," she said, forcing her words out. "You don't have to do this. Don't let what happened to you…make you a monster."

That laugh again. "It's a little late for that, Agent, don't you think? The true monsters are out there, hiding behind sweet smiles and pretty faces."

A crab started to crawl across Sadie's lower leg, and she suppressed a scream that turned into a whimper instead.

"You won't get away," she said, feeling tears sting her eyes. "They will see you…the Sheriff…"

"I know my way around this harbor in the dark," he told her. "They will never notice me leave. By the time they get to you, Agent, you and your friend here will be crab food. Sweet dreams." He turned and started to make his way back up the ladder, leaving her there.

Swiftly slipping into unconsciousness. In the dark. With the crabs.

Sudden terror flooded through her, but with it came a rush of adrenaline. With every last ounce of strength that she possessed, Sadie flung her whole body towards the wall, her eyes fixed on the life ring, even though she knew it meant throwing herself head long into the mass of the crabs.

Her fingers brushed the cord and she tried to grasp it, to pull, even as the fog enveloped her, dragging her down into oblivion. She heard him laughing at her once more and she gave one last, desperate sob as the darkness descended on her once again.

Her last thought before total sedation overtook her was that she had never found out what had really happened to Jessica.

And now it was too late.

CHAPTER THIRTY ONE

The Sheriff muttered under his breath as he jumped down from the private yacht onto the harbor, nearly losing his footing and falling into the icy water. Urgency was affecting his judgement.

It was the same story as before, except that the boats were far more luxurious and there were less people around to hinder their searches. Otherwise, search after search was turning up nothing. Cooper had been so certain that Agent Price's theory was right that he had half expected Emily or, at least, her body, to turn up straight away. As it was, they had been here nearly an hour and they were running out of boats to search.

He looked around him, staring into the distance. He could see the mountain ranges under the moonlight, rearing up on the horizon, and he had the sense of being watched. What if the killer was out there, somewhere close, watching them? Waiting for them to leave so he could dump Emily's body? They were going to have to keep guards stationed at both harbors until Emily turned up.

If Emily turned up. Price seemed to think the killer was too attached to his modus operandi to change it, even if it meant running the risk of getting caught, but what if she was wrong? People's behavior wasn't always predictable, and there was nothing about this guy that conformed to normality.

But there was nothing to do but continue the search.

Cooper was moving between piers, his flashlight illuminating the ground in front of him, when a sudden noise split the air.

A siren.

He started to run in the direction of the sound, reaching for his radio as he did so. Jane, down the other end of the harbor, came over the crackly line.

"Logan? What's that noise? Where's Sadie?"

He gave her a rough location and then radioed Price. There was nothing but crackling. He tried again, murmuring frantically under his breath. "Come on, Price, come in," he urged, feeling fear rise up in his chest.

Something had happened to her. To Sadie.

He reached the boat that the siren seemed to be emitting from, the *Lovely Lass*, and took a running jump onto the deck, landing in a crouch and whipping his gun out from the holster.

"Price!" he yelled. "If you're here, I need to know your location!"

As if by way of answer, the siren stopped abruptly, leaving a silence that seemed strangely loud in the absence of the ear-splitting noise. Cooper went very, very still, his gun held out before him as he looked around the deck and moved carefully forward. His skin prickled and he had the acute sense of being watched, and it wasn't by Agent Price.

He wondered how close Jane was to reaching the *Lovely Lass*, but he couldn't risk taking his attention away from his immediate surroundings to radio her.

The killer was here, watching him. Cooper could sense it, and with that knowledge came a throb of panic in his chest and he felt his mouth go dry.

The killer had got Sadie.

"Whoever you are," he said, keeping his voice calm. "I need you to show yourself, and with your hands in the air."

There was no response, but the air around him seemed to still as though it was listening to him. The only sound was the sea lapping at the side of the harbor.

He continued moving along the deck, then, sensing movement somewhere to his left, he swung in its direction.

"Stay where you are and put your hands above your head!" he yelled, but again there was no answer. He could hear his heart pounding in his chest, with terror for what might have happened to Sadie, and rage at the son of a bitch who would dare to harm her.

Then he heard a creaking sound. Shining the flashlight in its direction, he saw the entrance to the hold.

The hold. The place where the killer left his victims.

Holding his breath, Cooper made his way towards it, flinging the trap door back and stepping back, his gun at the ready, but no one emerged. He shone the flashlight down the hole, hearing the unmistakable scuttling of crabs. This was a boat that had not long been brought in, its catch left until the morning to be cleared out.

During which time, the crabs had plenty of opportunity to devour anything – anyone – that had been thrown into the hold with them.

The light shone on the crabs below and they moved furiously over each other to get out of its way. He felt sick at the thought of going down there among them but didn't hesitate. He lowered himself down onto the ladder, awkwardly facing outwards to climb down, his step precarious as he used the hand holding the flashlight to help himself down. It was awkward,- but turning his back on whoever might be down here could prove fatal.

"Price," he said over the noise of the crabs. "Are you in here?"

There was no answer, but at this point he wasn't really expecting one. He stumbled on the last rung of the ladder and had a horrible moment when he thought he would fall face first into the scrambling mass of crabs, but he managed to right himself at the last moment. Kicking crabs out of the way, he shone his light around the hold, searching frantically for a glimpse of either Sadie or Emily.

Then he saw a hand. Wading through the crabs towards it, he was about to start clearing crabs away from the body when he caught a movement from the corner of the hold in his peripheral vision. He pivoted towards it, but he was balancing on crabs and stumbled once more, just as he saw a man coming towards him with a pike raised over his head.

He lifted his gun, but he was out of time.

The pike hit him on the side of the head, and he stumbled sideways, falling into the pile of crustaceans. He shot his gun, but his fall caused the shot to go wide, just as the man rushed towards him with the pike held over his head. Cooper had dropped his flashlight and the beam of light bounced off the roof of the hold, but he could just make out the man's features as he loomed over him.

They were twisted with violent rage.

Cooper kicked out and the pike only glanced off his leg, but as he lifted his gun the man swung the weapon again, aiming for Cooper's pistol. He yelled in pain as the pike hit his wrist and the gun flew out of his hand and fell into the crabs, which were now starting to swarm over him, their pincers clicking.

The killer stood over him, a sneer on his face now as he raised the pike above his head and brought it down with deliberate force. He was aiming for a killing blow.

Cooper rolled sideways with all his strength, forcing his way through the crabs and reaching for his gun, which he could now only just glimpse through the heaving mass of crustacean bodies. As the killer brought the pike down into them, missing Cooper, he fell forward himself. Cooper kicked out at him, even though the awkward angle wrenched his muscles to do so, and he felt the stitches from his recent wound tear; but he was rewarded with a grunt of pain from the killer as Cooper's boot connected with his ribs.

Cooper frantically moved crabs aside, searching for his gun, and then saw that he was pushing them away from a slim and lightly tanned body that was already pitted with crab bites.

Emily. She looked still and felt cold, and there was no time for him to check for a pulse. He needed to get his gun.

He felt hands grab him from behind and rolled straight into the other man's fist. The guy was strong, and Cooper saw sparks behind his eyelids, but he was determined not to let the creep get the better of him. Shaking off the pain, he hit back, once and then again, making contact. Blood flew everywhere as the man's nose broke under his fist, but then Cooper slipped again on the moving floor underneath him and fell face first onto the crabs, only to feel the killer jump onto his back.

Cooper tried to buck the guy off from behind, but the man had his hands around Cooper's throat, squeezing with all his might, and Cooper felt himself choking. Summoning all his strength he bucked backwards, and though he didn't throw him off, the man's grip weakened. Cooper twisted to the side and used an old wrestling move he remembered from his jock days in senior high to slam the man sideways back into the crabs, causing the grip around his neck to be removed.

Seeing his chance, Cooper scrambled again for his gun, shoving crabs out of the way in an attempt to find it. Emily was still half uncovered, and, in the commotion, the crabs were clearly scared and thankfully seemed to be leaving her alone.

But where was Sadie?

His fingers closed around the gun, finally, but they also brushed something else.

Another body. With one sweep of his arm, he sent a bunch of crabs scattering and uncovered Sadie's head and torso. As yet she looked relatively unbitten, but she was also clearly unconscious.

"You goddamn bastard," Cooper snarled as he saw Sadie was naked and tied up, just like Emily. He tried to swing round with the gun then fell forward as he felt the killer land on his back again. The man was reaching over Cooper's head, going for the gun. He had a foot on Cooper's lower back, putting all of his weight onto his spine.

Cooper fought to keep hold of the gun and to turn around, so he was in a position to aim it at the man, but he was now face down in crabs. His hand closed over the trigger, but the other man's hand came down on top, trying to wrench the weapon from him. Cooper knew that even if he managed to shoot the gun now, he was running the risk of hitting either Emily or Sadie. He needed a clear shot.

They continued to wrestle, and Cooper gasped for air as he tried to turn around and keep the gun in his hand, which was now being wrenched painfully behind his back.

There was a loud crack that reverberated around the hold, causing Cooper's ears to ring, and the weight on his back had fallen away. The gun fell from his hand too, and Cooper wasn't sure who had pulled the trigger.

Had he been shot? He dragged himself to his feet and looked down to see the man falling backwards into the crabs, blood spreading across his chest and bubbling from his mouth.

The killer was dying.

But Cooper had no time for relief. He had to get Sadie and Emily out of there. As the crabs swarmed across the killer's body, scenting fresh blood, Cooper reached for Sadie, checking her pulse. She was alive.

Just.

"Logan!" Jane called from overhead, and then his sister's face appeared in the entrance to the hold. "What the hell?"

"Price is hurt. She's been drugged. Emily's here, but I'm not sure if she's dead or alive. I could use some help down here," he said, his voice weak. His stitches felt as though they were bleeding profusely, and he had torn a muscle in his shoulder, but there was no time to slow down.

Jane scrambled down the ladder and made straight for Emily.

"There's a pulse," she said, "But it's really weak. Let's get them on deck and we can call for an ambulance. We had better pray it gets here on time."

Between them they hauled both women up onto the deck, and then Jane radioed for an ambulance while Cooper loosened the bonds on both Emily and Sadie. Emily was freezing to the touch and Cooper took off his jacket and laid it over her, then gathered Sadie to him in an attempt to keep her warm too. He barely even registered the fact that she was naked in his arms.

He checked her pulse again to find it flickering. "Come on, Price," he said roughly, "Don't go and die on me now. Who else is going to tell me when I'm wrong?"

Feeling his sister's eyes on him, he looked up to see Jane watching him curiously, a knowing look in her gaze. She knew him too well.

"What?" he said defensively.

"You're fond of her Logan," she replied, her voice soft rather than accusing. "Aren't you?"

Cooper looked down at Sadie, noticing how long her eyelashes looked as they swept her too pale cheeks. "I suppose," he said gruffly. "We have been working together closely. She's a good cop."

"Yeah. She is," Jane said. "Don't tell her I said that, though."

Cooper tried to smile but he felt his stomach tighten with fear as he wondered if they would ever get the chance to. Just how long was the damn ambulance going to take?

He was about to voice the thought when he heard sirens and then saw lights sweeping the harbor. Breathing a sigh of relief, he lifted an arm and shouted over to them.

"You know," Jane said slowly, "it might be a good idea to never mention the fact that you were holding her while she had no clothes on either. She'll never forgive you."

"I was keeping her warm," he protested, but this time the corner of his mouth twitched. He could imagine the roasting that Sadie would give him right now if she knew.

He looked down at her, willing her to be okay. To pull through.

Just stay alive, Price, he said inside his own head. *And you can rage at me as much as you like*.

CHAPTER THIRTY TWO

The lights were too bright. Sadie blinked against them, trying to work out who had changed the usually dingy bulb in her motel room.

Then she remembered, and her eyes flew open, her hand automatically going to her waist for her gun.

"Lie down, dear," said a soothing voice above her. Her vision came into focus, and she saw a nurse above her, fiddling with an IV line which, she realized, was going straight into the back of her hand.

"How long have I been out?" she asked. Her voice was croaky, and her throat felt dry. She also had one hell of a headache.

"A couple of days. You missed Christmas; I hope you didn't have too many plans."

"I hadn't even thought about it," Sadie said honestly. She had assumed she would be working, turkey dinner with her father being out of the question.

"That's sad," the nurse said, giving her a sympathetic smile. "Especially when you have such devoted friends. I'll show them in while I go and get the doctor to check you over, although all your vitals are fine. I was beginning to wonder if you would sleep straight through New Year, too."

Sadie frowned as the nurse bustled off, wondering what she meant by friends. She hadn't been back here long enough to really make any, certainly not the sort that would be waiting by her hospital room for her to wake up.

Yet she found she wasn't that surprised when the Sheriff and his sister walked in, the relief at seeing her awake and well written large on their faces.

"Thank God," the Deputy said with a grin. "We thought we had lost you there for a minute. Then we would have to put up with another of Golightly's FBI stars all over our patch."

Sadie chuckled weakly. "I'm glad I could be of service to you guys," she joked. Then she looked at Cooper, feeling almost shy to meet his gaze, although if she had been asked, she wouldn't have been able to explain why.

"We must stop meeting in hospital rooms like this," she said as Cooper took the seat next to her bed. He looked tired, as though he had been up for days, and she wondered just how long he had been here, waiting to see if she was okay.

"Yeah, I could do without seeing another one for a while," he said. "I had to get my stitches sewn back up when we brought you in."

"Oh? By that nice redhead again?" Sadie asked, raising an eyebrow.

"No, some guy with blue hair. You get all sorts these days," he said with a smile. His eyes were warm as he looked at her.

"On a serious note, what happened?" Sadie said. "Emily? Is she…?"

"She's okay," Jane cut in. "She actually came around before you did…the nurse said you had a really bad reaction to the diazepam. The bites on her body were mostly superficial, so the crabs hadn't yet done too much damage. But her tongue, well, she won't be able to speak fully again. But she's alive, Sadie, that's the main thing," she said hurriedly, noticing the look on Sadie's face. "We did all we could."

"And you nearly died, too," Cooper said, his face taking on a haunted look as he remembered the events that Sadie had been out cold for. "We should never have split up."

"If we hadn't," Sadie argued, "we might never have got to Emily in time. Or apprehended the killer. Who is he?"

Cooper hesitated. "Who *was* he," he corrected. "I shot him. I heard your siren and came to find you, and he surprised me in the hold and attacked me with a pike. There was a struggle. To be honest, I'm not entirely sure which one of us pulled the trigger, but it was him that the bullet hit."

Thank God, Sadie thought, hoping that Cooper didn't feel guilty. She wondered if the dockhand was the first person that he had killed in the line of duty.

The first one was always the hardest.

Then she suddenly sat straight up in bed, pulling at the IV in her hand.

"Whoa!" Cooper said, reaching for her. "What the hell are you doing, Price?"

"It's the day after Boxing Day, right? I'm supposed to be in Washington. I have to be at Quantico tomorrow." She looked around her frantically for a button to call the nurse back. "I have to get out of here."

"Calm down," Jane said in a soothing voice, "It's fine, Sadie."

"You don't understand," Sadie protested, but Cooper cut her off.

"Golightly called and set to let you know that he had sorted it," he told her. "It will be rescheduled. You don't need to go anywhere."

Sadie lay back on the pillows, trying to take in the news. She had a brief reprieve, but that also meant that Golightly did know about the hearing after all, which meant that at some point, he was going to want to know the details.

"Whatever it is," Cooper said, seeing her expression, "It can wait for now, Price."

"I still need to get out of here," Sadie groaned. "I hate hospitals."

She heard footsteps coming into the room and looked around, ready to tell the doctor that she wanted to be discharged as soon as he had checked her over. She felt groggy, but she was fine.

Except it wasn't the doctor. It was Caz, a big smile across her face, holding a huge bouquet of flowers in one hand and Jenny's hand in the other. Sadie felt sudden tears sting her eyes as the little girl let go of her mother and ran over to her, throwing her arms around Sadie's neck.

"Thank you," Jenny whispered to her. "Thank you for saving Emily."

"It's okay sweetie," Sadie whispered into the girl's hair, which smelled of watermelon. A tear hit her cheek and she wiped it away with the back of her hand.

The drugs must be making her emotional.

"Hey, Agent Price," Caz said. The Sheriff stood up and offered her his chair, taking the flowers from her.

"I'll go and find some water for these," he said.

"Find the doctor," Sadie called after him. "I want to get out of here. They're beautiful," she said, turning to Caz. "Thank you." She blinked rapidly, worried that she was about to start to cry again.

"Thank you," Caz said. "Emily would be dead if it wasn't for you."

"I just wish she wasn't harmed," Sadie whispered, not wanting to say too much to Jenny. Caz nodded soberly.

"I know. But she'll get through it. Her parents have flown over, and I suspect that she'll go back with them. I guess I'll need a new au pair."

There was a silence in the room for a moment, which was broken by the arrival of the doctor, the Sheriff behind him.

"We'll wait outside while the doctor does your observations," Caz said, getting up. "And by the way, your next drink is on the house. For the foreseeable future." She winked at Sadie. "So, I'll be stocking up on that whiskey you like."

Sadie grimaced. Suddenly, she couldn't think of anything worse. "Make it soft drinks," she said. "I'm off the hard stuff…for the foreseeable future."

They exchanged a smile as Caz walked out, followed by the others, and Sadie lay back on her pillow. Everything, for now, was fine. Emily was alive, the killer was dead, and her hearing had been postponed. For a few days at least, she had nothing to worry about and nothing to do.

Except for one thing.

Which was long overdue.

Her father.

CHAPTER THIRTY THREE

Sadie walked up the path to her father's door, her chin held high with determination. This time, she wasn't about to take no for an answer, or let him turn her away again. This time, she had new knowledge, and she wasn't going anywhere until her father told her the things that she needed to know.

Things that had been kept secret for far too long.

If this last case had taught her anything, it was that secrets were always better brought out into the light. If the murdering dockhand, who had turned out to go by the name of Adam Gillespie, had been able to tell the secret of his abuse to someone who had believed him, Carmen and Dana might still be alive, and Emily might still have her mouth intact.

And if Carmen and Dana and all the other accomplices hadn't been able to manipulate the kids in their care into keeping secrets, Silverman would have been behind bars sooner.

Both cases were out in the press now, and Anchorage was dealing with the shock of discovering the secrets in its midst. As more details came out about both Adam's past and Silverman's trafficking ring, it became apparent just how well evil could flourish in the silence of the secrets that people kept.

Sadie wasn't going to allow her father the privilege of his silence anymore. She owed it to her sister to find out what had happened to her.

She banged the door of her father's rundown cabin loudly, and then stood back and waited. In her other hand, she held the folder that Sheriff Cooper had given her before she had left the Station to drive here. The file that held all the details of Jessica's case, including that mysterious phone call from her father.

They took her.

Who? Who took her? It was time he told the truth about that day. Squaring her shoulders, Sadie banged the door again.

"Who is it?" his voice yelled, just as Sadie saw the curtain in the window twitch. He knew damn well that it was her. Even so, she answered him.

"It's me, Dad," she yelled, although the word stuck in her throat. He had long lost the right to be called that by her. "It's Sadie."

There was a silence. She banged the door again. "I'm not going anywhere," she yelled, "Until you answer this goddamn door."

Finally, she heard his footsteps coming towards the door, and she held herself still as she heard the bolts slide back. For just a second, she was a frightened kid again, fearing the wrath of her father but determined not to show it. Then she took a deep breath, and the moment passed.

She wasn't a kid anymore. She was a Special Agent, an expert in her field, who had gotten further and achieved more than her father would have believed, and she had done it alone and without his help. There was nothing to be scared of anymore.

When the door cracked open and his face appeared, her first thought was how ill he looked. His doctor had told her that he had terminal cancer, and right now it showed, He had lost weight, his skin was wrinkly and tinged with gray, his eyes rheumy and with bloodshot irises.

She could smell the booze on him too. Some things never changed.

For all his pitiful appearance however, his eyes burned with something like his old malevolence.

"I told you to go away," he said, spitting out his words. "Why are you back here? Leave an old man in peace, why can't you?"

Sadie almost wanted to laugh at the self-pity inherent in his words. "Sorry, Dad, no can do," she said. "I need to talk to you, and you are going to talk to me. It's been too long."

He snorted. "Not long enough," he said. "What are you doing back here? I saw you in the news," he added, but his tone was accusatory, as though he thought that she had returned simply to spite him.

Perhaps, on some level, she had.

"I had a job to do," she said.

"Go and do it, then," he spat. "What do you want with me? Turning up here after all this time, after no word for years."

Sadie shook her head, wondering just what story he was telling himself where he had somehow managed to end up as the victim in their family situation. She didn't have time for this.

“I’m not here about me and you, Dad,” she said. “I have questions to ask you. And if I have to haul your ass down to Sheriff Cooper’s station to get you to answer them, then I swear to God that’s exactly what I’ll do.”

He glared at her, but Sadie met his gaze head on. She saw him flinch as though in surprise as he realized that she really wasn’t scared of him anymore, and that he couldn’t intimidate her anymore. Then his eyes dropped to the folder in her hand, and they went wide.

“What is that?” he said, but she could tell that he had already guessed exactly what it was. This day was always going to come; Sadie could see it now.

Secrets always had to come into the light.

“It’s Jessica’s file, Dad,” she told him, watching him closely for his reaction.

“What do you want with that? Your sister’s dead. Why torment me with it now?”

Sadie had to swallow her rage. *Torment you*? She wanted to scream at him. It had been her that had been left with the nightmares, the questions and the grief, while he continued to drink himself to death.

But she said none of that. Instead, she lifted up the file. “Some…discrepancies have come to light,” she said coolly. “We’re reopening the case. And you’re going to talk to me.”

He went to slam the door in her face once again, but this time Sadie was expecting it and was too quick for him. He looked down in surprise at Sadie’s leather-booted foot wedged in between the door and the frame.

“Let me in,” she said. He stared at her, hatred and fear in his eyes.

Then he opened the door.

NOW AVAILABLE!

ONLY HIS
(A Sadie Price FBI Suspense Thriller—Book 3)

ONLY HIS (A Sadie Price FBI Suspense Thriller) is book #3 in a chilling new series by mystery and thriller author Rylie Dark, which begins with ONLY MURDER (book #1).

Special Agent Sadie Price, a 29-year-old rising star in the FBI's BAU unit, stuns her colleagues by requesting reassignment to the FBI's remote Alaskan field office. Back in her home state, a place she vowed she would never return, Sadie, running from a secret in her recent past and back into her old one, finds herself facing her demons—including her sister's unsolved murder—while assigned to hunt down a new serial killer.

When a young woman is found mauled by a bear—the second case in one week—the authorities chalk it up to a desperate animal, driven by hunger to attack. Nature, as far as the locals are concerned, can be as cruel a killer as any murderer.

But Sadie isn't convinced. She suspects a serial killer, and when she realizes both victims were young women living alone in cabins, she takes it upon herself to visit a string of isolated, desolate cabins in the wilderness, including one with particular significance—her father's.

When a third woman is found, Sadie knows she is the only thing standing between this diabolical killer and his innocent, next victim.

But in the forbidding wilderness, in the thick of winter, can Sadie reach the woman before it's too late? And can she stop this killer all while unearthing the ghosts of her own family's past?

An action-packed page-turner, the SADIE PRICE series is a riveting crime thriller, jammed with suspense, surprises and twists and turns that you won't see coming. It will have you fall in love with a brilliant and scarred new character, while challenging you, amidst a barren landscape, to solve an impenetrable crime.

Books #4-#6 in the series—ONLY ONCE, ONLY SPITE, and ONLY MADNESS—are also available.

Rylie Dark

Debut author Rylie Dark is author of the SADIE PRICE FBI SUSPENSE THRILLER series, comprising six books (and counting); the MIA NORTH FBI SUSPENSE THRILLER series, comprising three books (and counting); and the CARLY SEE FBI SUSPENSE THRILLER, comprising three books (and counting).

An avid reader and lifelong fan of the mystery and thriller genres, Rylie loves to hear from you, so please feel free to visit www.ryliedark.com to learn more and stay in touch.

BOOKS BY RYLIE DARK

SADIE PRICE FBI SUSPENSE THRILLER
ONLY MURDER (Book #1)
ONLY RAGE (Book #2)
ONLY HIS (Book #3)
ONLY ONCE (Book #4)
ONLY SPITE (Book #5)
ONLY MADNESS (Book #6)

MIA NORTH FBI SUSPENSE THRILLER
NO WAY OUT (Book #1)
NO WAY BACK (Book #2)
NO WAY HOME (Book #3)

CARLY SEE FBI SUSPENSE THRILLER
NO WAY OUT (Book #1)
NO WAY BACK (Book #2)
NO WAY HOME (Book #3)

www.ingramcontent.com/pod-product-compliance
Lightning Source LLC
Chambersburg PA
CBHW030614310726
48979CB00003B/713

* 9 7 8 1 0 9 4 3 9 3 2 8 5 *